Spell Hath No Fury

FATE WEAVER
BOOK FIVE

REGINA WELLING

Spell Hath No Fury

ISBN- 978-1-953044-04-4

Cover design by: L. Vryhof
Interior design by: L. Vryhof

http://reginawelling.com
http://erinlynnwrites.com

First Edition
Printed in the U.S.A.

Contents

Chapter 1 1
Chapter 2 18
Chapter 3 34
Chapter 4 44
Chapter 5 55
Chapter 6 61
Chapter 7 73
Chapter 8 91
Chapter 9 106
Chapter 10 116
Chapter 11 124
Chapter 12 132
Chapter 13 144
Chapter 14 151
Chapter 15 167
Chapter 16 178
Chapter 17 184
Chapter 18 194
Chapter 19 209
Chapter 20 221
Chapter 21 245
Chapter 22 250
Chapter 23 254

Chapter 1

"Are you all right?" Someone shook my shoulder. "Miss, are you all right?" The strange man's garlic-and-onion breath made an effective substitute for smelling salts.

"What happened?" My head pounded to the beat of my heart, and when I sat up, the world spun once, then twice. My questing fingers probed the throbbing spot and settled on a lump near my temple.

"You slammed right into that trash bin. You were just walking right along and then bam! Next time, you should look where you're going."

But I like a good concussion, Captain Obvious. I summoned the retort but was too dazed to bother saying it out loud. His good deed done for the day, my Samaritan heaved himself to standing, patted the sparse hairs of his up-and-over style back into place and left me to my misery.

If anyone had ever told me taking over for my father and playing Cupid would turn me into a glorified, full-time stalker, I'd have refused the job. Not that anyone asked me if I wanted it in the first place.

And now my target had fled.

As if I didn't already know I'd missed the mark, the Bow of Destiny blatted a note of displeasure in my head, and I had to hold back a shriek of pain as the sound ricocheted off the inside of my sore skull.

"Give it a rest, will you?" I clutched my aching head.

Box after box of chocolates fly off the shelves every February with cute little angels plastered all over their shiny redness. Too bad the candy makers completely missed the mark when it came to decorating. My dad was no winged cherub holding some adorable little bow with heart-tipped arrows.

I mean, the heart-shaped arrow was right, but the cute baby part was all wrong. Nope, Cupid was a man. Or technically a god, but he looked like a man. One I'd never met, and one who forged his bow—a serious weapon—from living gold.

Living. Gold. As in gold that lived. *And where did it live?* you might ask. Inside me, that's where.

Moreover, the stupid thing had a brain of sorts, and an opinion on everything that had to do with my work. One it liked to share musically. At a high volume.

Fishing around in the messenger bag I'd been using

for a purse, I pulled out a bottle containing the dregs of my faerie godmother's restorative elixir, and downed the last few drops. Like magic—because it *was* magic—the potion dispelled half the headache. Pain faded away, taking most of the fuzzy thoughts with it, temporarily at least.

A stay of execution so I could finish my job. In a few hours, I'd pay for messing with the natural order of things, though.

Magic always comes with a price.

The next magical flourish of sound only made me wince. I considered that progress.

"I'll go find whoever it is. Are you happy now?"

From the outside, talking to the bow looked a lot like talking to myself. The answer came in the form of a cheery tune as I staggered out of the mouth of the alley and loped down the sidewalk.

A moment of concentration reactivated the weapon's sight. Like something out of a superhero movie, a circle with a set of crosshairs hovered just ahead of my right eye. My imagination supplied robotic sound effects every time I blinked and the focus altered.

All I needed now was a pink spandex suit with a symbol splashed across the chest. Lexi Balefire: Matchwoman. No, that didn't sound right. Lovemaker? Ugh. Worse, and with a vaguely dirty undertone. Matchwitch was a little closer, but maybe I'd better leave the superhero name thing alone for the time being.

Armed and ready, I locked in on the place in my gut that always knew where to find potential lovers. Cars have GPS, I have LPS—an internal Love Positioning System.

The pull was strong this time. Anticipation stole my breath like I'd crested the hill on a roller coaster, caught in that moment of foreboding just before the awful plunge. This match felt epic and desperate to be made. Not normal, in other words.

Even without Terra's magic healing juice lending me artificial strength, I would have hurried forward, the compulsion was so strong. My date with the dumpster had cost me valuable time and, according to the intensity of the pull, I had only seconds to make this work, so I kicked the pace up another notch.

Nerves jittered as I closed in on my quarry. My stomach lurched when the target symbol finally blinked red and split into two. One crossed circle oriented on a man walking away from me, the other on a woman walking toward. A complicated orchestral arrangement sounded in my head—at a volume that would have made my ears ring, but made my skull bones vibrate instead.

A simple ta-da *would have worked, do you have to make a big deal out of everything?* I thought at the bow.

It blew a musical raspberry at me in response.

In a cloud of glowing light, the bow-carrying inner Goddess—the part of me with the power to handle my father's weapon—stepped forward, and with a practiced hand brought the Bow of Destiny to bear. She looked like me except for the hair. Mine, a nut-brown riot of curls shot through with strands of copper, hers a slanting wing of white tipped with neon pink. Oh, and the eyes were different, too. Pink and piercing, she fixed hers upon the two unsuspecting hearts, took aim, and fired.

A pair of arrows zinged toward their targets.

Now you're just showing off. I actually felt her smirk on my face as she faded away, and I turned my attention back to the couple. Moments like these were what I loved most about my job; the part where I watched two halves of one soul come together.

The impact of arrow to heart makes no sound, and I'm the only one who ever flinches, but that's just because I can see the tip slice bloodlessly through flesh and bone. Then comes that delicious moment when eyes lock and fates poise right on the edge of being sealed.

Matches made by the Bow of Destiny last forever. They embody the ideals set out in traditional marriage vows: in sickness and in health, forsaking all others. One hundred percent fated, a done deal. Never to be put asunder. Odd word choice, but it fits.

I work on a sliding scale of love, and yes, I know how ridiculous that sounds.

For instance, most of the couples I bring together using the tried-and-true methods employed at FootSwept, my matchmaking business, experience true love's kiss. On the hundred point scale of longevity, these matches come in at a solid ninety. It's rare for a TLK match to turn bad, but it happens.

A fact I'd learned only recently.

This couple, according to my gut and my heart, would hit the scale at ten times the going rate. Their love mojo was strong. Off the charts. Fated.

But if they were fated, why did they need and my living arrows, you ask?

Simple.

It's all about the math.

One hundred percent is better than ninety, and since my senses insisted this couple's union carried an air of heightened significance, I used an arrow to close the gap, leaving nothing to chance.

Some soul mates are a drop in the bucket that rests on the scales of human emotion; others are a hurricane-level downpour. Both help keep the balance of good and evil in check, and none are inconsequential. Love really does make the world go around.

At least, that's the impression I'd gathered during my time with the illustrious bow. To my everlasting annoyance, it had come without instructions or explanations. I was too lowly a peon in the hierarchy of my father's world for anyone to bother cluing me in. About anything, really.

Maybe the force of their destiny would have eventually drawn the couple together without my interference, but the bow wanted them matched. Right now. And since it wouldn't shut up, I fired the arrows and did the deed. Or the pink-eyed part of me I considered to be my inner goddess did. At any rate, the job was done..

It would have been nice to know the new lover's names at least.

The goddess part of me, my father's true legacy, might have been a source of information, but she wasn't talking. All pink and glowing, she popped out just long enough to do the shooting, then faded back into the recesses of my being like one part of a multiple personality. Her communication skills left a lot to be desired. Up to now, she'd done little more than a wag finger at me when I tried to override her will with my own intuition.

The other half of my genetic makeup is pure witch. I come from a long line of magically powerful women. From what I knew of him, our strong blood magic is what attracted Cupid to my mother. Daddy has a reputation for spreading the love, and since him making babies with witches yielded Fate Weavers like me, it made sense he'd have been drawn to one with a lot of power.

Whatever my personal issues—and they abounded—my attention refocused on the couple when they locked eyes and turned the street into something right out of musical theater. Okay, maybe I was the only one with a romantic soundtrack playing in my head when the man and woman came together, but as an audience of one, I can tell you there wasn't a dry eye in the house.

Drawn as if by a powerful, magnetic force, the lovers stopped with less than a foot of distance between them. Circling left, I sank down on a convenient bench where I could see and hear everything.

Nosy? Me? Guilty as charged.

"Didn't we meet at the…" He said.

She aimed a shy smile at him, "…Old Port Festival. You were selling…"

"…Blown glass ornaments and you…"

"…Bought one for my mother, and then came back and bought three more for…"

"…Your sisters, but I knew they were for you the whole time."

Oh, how cute, they were already finishing each other's sentences and little hearts and stars formed over their heads.

Actual hearts and stars, mind you. The glowing kind that are probably some kind of code telling me something about the match. Again, no instructions came with my abilities and if there was a pattern here, I couldn't make perfect sense of it.

This was the moment that made romance novels fly off the shelves and sparked love songs about two hearts beating as one.

The wave of new love spread like rings of water

around a stone thrown into a calm lake. Out from this place, through the city and beyond, it left everything in its path a little sweeter, slightly cleaner than before. Until, with a jarring shudder, the circle of power struck an opposing force.

A force filled with fury.

Fury and pain that rumbled back toward me, threatened to flood me with dark emotion meant to steal away my newfound joy. My head rang when the bow answered with a song of power and rival strength.

Something—or someone—out there wanted to test its darkness against my light, wanted to subvert hope, remove love from the world—and it didn't care if it took me out in the process. My death would be a fine feather in its cap.

Oh goodie, Lexi Balefire, matchmaking witch has an enemy. It must be Tuesday.

"How do my legs look in these boots? Good enough to welcome Kin back home with a bang?" I asked Flix as he cleaned up follonwing a cut-and-color in the salon adjacent to the massive closet in the back of the FootSwept office.

"You've got the gams, girl. But the footwear is a little last season, don't you think?"

"Is it?" I twisted my leg so see the way the boot fit my foot. "I haven't had time to do any headhunting for

Neimans in months." I grouched, remembering the days when it was a job in itself to find room on the racks for one of their gratis shipments. Being a full-fledged Fate Weaver wasn't just affecting my life, it was affecting my fashion sense.

My skills, while best at matching lovers, could easily have earned me a solid upper-level income as a corporate headhunter. Sometimes I wonder how my life would have turned out if I'd gone that route instead of opening a business many consider one shallow step above a dating service.

With love as my focus, I moonlighted a little on the side and took my payment in free merchandise that I often passed on to those of my clients who need a little confidence boost.

We didn't make over every seeker of love that walked through the front doors; just the ones who needed a little extra attention or some aggressive pampering. Nobody, and I mean nobody, can fail to feel sexy while wearing a pair of Manolo Blahniks.

You'd be surprised at how many first kisses have been instigated by the stiletto heel.

I was not doodling Kin Clark, my boyfriend's name, surrounded by hearts and arrows half an hour later when the phone rang. That would be undignified.

"Lexi? It's Yvonne Hightower. I'm—this isn't easy—I've been thinking, and I've decided I no longer require your services."

She had my full attention.

"Are you sure?" I'd already found her perfect match, and it was a strong one. The kind that made the Bow of Destiny lilt a sprightly tune in my head. Perhaps not as loud or complex a tune as the one it played for the couple I'd matched the day before, but happy enough.

"I'm sorry, I really am, but I'm sure."

"If it's the fee, I'm happy to give you the friends and family discount." Money wasn't my main reason for mating lonely couples—or even in the top ten. Matchmaking was in my genes. With Cupid for a father, what else would I do? It's the family business, and I'd been doing it since before I knew it literally ran in my blood.

Except lately, my business had been experiencing a series of mood swings. I was either swamped or hearing crickets with no happy medium to be found, and at the moment, the chirping was about to drive me nuts.

Okay, I'd admit to having been a little distracted the past few weeks. While fate weaving and the work I did at FootSwept were similar in nature, they didn't mesh quite as seamlessly as you'd think. In theory, I could just shoot everyone who came in the door, or sit on a busy corner, and BAM, match the entire city in a matter of days.

While I had no actual assurance I was right, I thought there was a reason why the bow only targeted certain individuals. As wonderful as love is, you can't force it down someone's throat if they're not ready.

Take me, for instance. I think if I'd met my boyfriend five years earlier, I wouldn't have been ready to be Kin's soul mate, and I'd be willing to bet the same applies to many of the couples I've matched. Not all of my recent clients popped up with a set of glowing symbols over their heads—my sign to use the bow. The dichotomy was another of the intricacies I hadn't quite figured out yet.

Maybe the couple needed more time or maybe it was me who wasn't ready. Weaving fates is a work in progress.

"Thank you, but no." Yvonne sounded faintly embarrassed, and common sense urged me to just hang up before I made an even bigger fool out of myself. What does common sense know?

"Was it something I said?" Resorting to clichés—not proud of it.

"I've decided to go with Diana Diamond." The soft click of the disconnected line ended the conversation.

Diana Diamond, the self-styled queen of hearts.

With her face splashed all over billboards and buses and late-night TV, Diana pulled in the desperate and lonely with promises of matches that would make their hearts—and other things—go pitter-patter. People were lining up to see if she really could find their "diamond in the rough."

During one of my glut periods, I'd been thankful

she was taking up the slack. Now it seemed like she might be expanding a little too deeply into my customer base. Sour grapes make lousy wine—or is that whine?   I didn't want to be that person, but Yvonne was the fourth client in three weeks to call and politely take their business elsewhere.

One client didn't worry me. People have different tastes; it made sense some would prefer her style over mine. Then a second and a third until Yvonne removed the last of my doubts. Diana was poaching my clients—picking them off one by one. Probably my own fault to some degree, considering how distracted I'd been since becoming a full-fledged witch.

Fortunately for her, I was born a good witch and not a wicked one because the temptation to hex all Diana's clothes a size too small was strong. Or pimples. Pimples were good.

Being the bigger person was only half the reason I restrained myself. The other half had to do with knowing the spirit of whatever I sent out would come back to me times three. Yvonne getting her match was what counted, right? Not revenge against the client-poaching tramp who made it happen.

Still, it rankled.

"Who peed in your Cheerios?" Flix, my business partner and best friend, asked with a furrowed brow as he winked into the room.

Faeries—even half-Fae—have the super cool

ability to transport themselves through space instantly. We witches have to work a lot harder to achieve the same effect. My attempts at skimming distance had been pathetic failures. That rankled, too.

"Yvonne Hightower just fired me. Us. And I'll give you two guesses whose services she intends to employ now."

Flix settled onto one of the Chippendale chairs opposite my desk and crossed one perfectly-sculpted, designer jean-clad leg over the other.

Considering himself the epitome of manly perfection, Flix had cropped his platinum blond hair short and styled it into intentionally mussed spikes. Toned and tanned biceps were not the product of curls and dead lifts in the gym, his Fae genetics negated the need to work out. His gym membership had, I suspected, until recently provided an excuse to troll for hot, equally-muscled men. Lately, he'd found someone to love, and I couldn't be happier for him.

Still, he'd never asked me if Carl was his soul mate, and out of deference, I hadn't looked.

"What do you know about this woman? Is she like you? Another Fate Weaver, I mean." Flix raised an eyebrow and voiced the question I'd been pondering for weeks.

"No idea. I've never laid eyes on her in person. Seen her ads on TV and didn't get the tingle. Which means she's probably no better than a dating app. I'd almost rather she *was* another half-sibling; at least then she'd have the aptitude, and I wouldn't be worried that my more fickle clients were going to miss out on true love."

I sighed and threw myself an internal pity party while imagining Diana Diamond losing clients by the dozen. She'd go broke and slink away in misery to leave all the lovers in town for me. "Strikes me as a fake from roots to boots. Or maybe I'm being dramatic."

"Well, that is your default setting, Lexi darling. But that doesn't mean you're wrong. Carl says we don't trust our instincts enough anymore; we ignore physical cues and focus too much on society's expectation of treating everyone as equals. It's become politically incorrect to simply not like someone for no apparent reason, but really it's nature's way of letting us know when something isn't right."

"Sounds like a good enough justification for judgmental bitchiness. I'll take it." I laughed.

"See, having a professor of anthropology in the family has its benefits. Plus, Carl looks hot in those jackets with the suede elbow patches. Win-win."

I rolled my eyes but couldn't hold back a grin. Flix and I were still getting over our worst fight ever, and he'd finally come back to work after an extended vacation. Left without their favorite hairstylist, his regular clients pestered me day in and day out. Since his return, the salon in the back of the office needed a revolving door.

I heard one harried woman offer him the diamond pendant she was wearing if he'd skip lunch to do her highlights. I'm *pretty* sure he declined.

"You like your elbow patches; I like my man with a guitar in his hand. Whatever floats your boat."

"When is your rock star boyfriend coming back to town, anyway? Mona Katz keeps calling about setting up a double date."

"He's not a rock star. Yet. And I hope he never becomes one. He's just filling in for Rain of Thirteen's guitarist while they find a permanent replacement. He'll be back in a few days, and I'll call Mona then. Otherwise, I'll never get her off the phone."

I'd begun to wonder if Kin had caught the travel bug during his trip, which was originally slated to last four weeks but had dragged on for another two and was now threatening to eclipse the Thanksgiving holiday.

There was no point setting up a dinner with Mona and her boyfriend if he got delayed again because it increased the chances of her forcing a heart-to-heart talk over my feelings. I didn't want to talk about the tour. Or Kin. Or anything else, for that matter. Not yet, anyway.

Kin hadn't seemed particularly enthused about the idea of extending our separation, but he'd been making good contacts on the tour, so I'd pasted a smile on my face and acted like I was happy for him. Flix knew better. Mona would have, too, and that's precisely why

I'd been avoiding her calls.

"You're radiating fear, and I can smell the freakout oozing from your pores. I don't know why you try to lie to a faerie—especially me, considering I know you better than anyone on the planet." Extreme empathy was one of Flix's gifts. Or maybe it was a curse, I hadn't ever asked because, while a little too open about his romantic entanglements, he tended to clam up about certain personal details.

"Turn off your spidey senses or whatever you want to call them. We're not having this conversation now. Everything will be fine." Avoiding making eye contact for fear I might prove him right and burst into tears, I reiterated.

It might seem like I had more going for me than most people—I'm a witch, the demigod daughter of Cupid, Keeper of the sacred Balefire flame, and last but not least, a Fate Weaver. But damn it all, I still cared more about the one title that had nothing to do with my supernaturally-enhanced world: girlfriend.

"Whatever you say, Lexi. Whatever you say."

Chapter 2

"Phone tag. You're it." Kin's husky drawl warmed my voicemail box. "I'm in…Baltimore, I think. It's hard to keep track, and it feels like a hundred years since I've seen your beautiful face. Wish you'd have picked up. I miss you, babe. Counting the days."

I played the message a second time. Figures Kin's call would come in just as I walked into the business that housed the one and only dead cell spot in the entire city of Port Harbor. Five minutes to pick up a sandwich left just enough to miss him again because when I returned the call, it went straight to his voicemail.

"Me, too. Counting the days, I mean. I miss you so much. Call me later, I promise to stay out of Deli Delight until you come back. Love you."

What I wanted more than anything in the world was to skip up Kin's front steps and throw my arms around him, but his windows were dark and empty.

Thankfully, there was one other person who needed my help, and who would provide a much-needed distraction. I turned toward the one place no one who knew me well would ever expect me to go.

The home of my sworn enemy, Serena Snodgrass.

Technically, we weren't enemies anymore, but even if our relationship had entered an uneasy truce, I wouldn't call us fast friends. Joining up to defend against a rogue witch with a demented pet could cure even the most tumultuous of relationships. And Serena had been my best friend once upon a time—probably precisely why we'd been so hard on each other over the years.

"I'm glad to see you. What took you so long?" Serena asked warily. I blamed hormones for the flip-flop between gratefulness and snark. "I called hours ago, and I'm really freaking out here."

"I'm sorry, but haven't you ever heard of work? I do have a job, you know." How long I could keep saying that was anyone's guess, and as soon as the words left my mouth, I felt like a jerk for snapping at a pregnant woman. "Sorry. I keep forgetting I don't hate you anymore. I hope you're still having those tuna and pickle cravings because I brought you a sandwich."

A lukewarm apology, but it would have to do. Serena didn't seem terribly concerned and our verbal sparring matches hadn't stopped just because we were about to become inextricably linked.

My good for nothing half-brother Jett being the father of her baby meant I had new family on the way. The jerk had no idea he would become a dad in a few months, and as far as I was concerned, Serena was better off without him.

Bitter about a family history I'd had nothing to do with, Jett had taken his wrath out on me before I even knew we were related. I could forgive him that if he hadn't chosen Kin as his pawn in the battle not once but twice.

The second episode of my family saga landed Carl in danger and had Flix sending Jett on what was supposed to be a permanent vacation to the Faelands. Recently, we learned Jett had managed to escape his banishment weeks before and hadn't even notified Serena of his return.

"Thanks, I'm starved. All the time, actually. I swear this baby is going to be twelve pounds the way she's going." Serena bit into the sandwich and closed her eyes as though tasting the nectar of the gods.

"Is it a girl for sure?" Female witch births outnumbered male by a large margin, but I had no idea whether the same could be said for babies born to demigods and witches.

"No idea." Serena got a jar of mini gherkins from the fridge, added two more to her sandwich. "Don't tell anyone in the coven, but I went in for an ultrasound because I wanted, you know, visual proof and the doctor couldn't seem to get a good enough look. Whatever is in there has a highly developed sense of modesty to go along with the weird cravings."

"You know, impending motherhood agrees with you." On Serena's formerly rail-thin frame, the added pounds showed off a more rounded figure and filled out her narrow face.

"Thanks." I could almost smell the curiosity coming off her, but only an arched eyebrow indicated skepticism, and she decided to let the compliment pass.

I watched her put away the sandwich in no time flat, then Serena rose to retrieve an elaborately-decorated potion bottle from a narrow cabinet between the stove and refrigerator.

"Before I forget, I've got something for your grandmother. She sent this over to help with the morning sickness, and I have to tell you, it was a minor miracle." Strong emotions shadowed her face. "Right when I needed one most. Thank her for me, won't you?"

Serena's hands quivered as she laid the bottle on the table beside me, her expression twisted into one I assessed as miserable and scared before she crossed the room to stare out the window. "How did she get through it?"

"Who?" Rising, I circled the table to gently put an arm around her waist and lead her back to her chair.

Seated across from Serena, I waited.

"Your mother. I mean, you're a demigod," in the

past, she would have let acid coat the word as it dripped off her tongue, but today she kept her tone neutral. "How bad was it? I need to know."

To me, the question was clear as three-day-old coffee—my mother might have understood what Serena was asking, but she wasn't around to consult. I'd run Sylvana off the day she made the grave mistake of nearly letting my boyfriend die. I'd expected as much from an enemy like Jett, but my mother's betrayal had cut deep. We hadn't taken time to bond over stories of my early babyhood.

"I don't know what you're asking, and even if she were here, I wouldn't believe her if she told me the sky was blue. How bad was what?"

"The birth, you idiot." There was a taste of the old Serena. "You know it's more than a normal magical birth, right? There are protocols for these things: spells, incantations, protections to be put in place. One mistake could cost me everything; my life, the baby. Everything."

"Really? Gran never mentioned anything like that to me." Oversight, or another family mystery no one thought Lexi should know about?

Arms wrapped around her waist, Serena rocked back and forth. "Clara says I shouldn't worry, she and Mag have been through it before, but I can't stop that scene from Alien playing in my head. I'm scared to death. Can you talk to her for me? See if she'll give you more details? Anything to set my mind at rest."

Reaching across the table, I curled my fingers around hers, gave them a squeeze and tried to transfer a little of my warmth to her chilled flesh. Serena was asking me to do the one thing I'd been trying to avoid ever since I'd found out Jett was back from the Faelands—bring up his name to my family.

How could I say no?

"I will. But if she says she has a plan for helping you through this, you can trust her. Gran's nothing like my mother."

Well, in looks, they were nearly identical, but I meant in spirit. "Try to put it out of your mind, for now, all this worry can't be good for the baby."

"See, there's another problem, and it's the reason I called you today. Here's the list Clara sent over, and I'm supposed to gather all these things to assist with the birth. Problem is, I can't find the most important item—my family's talisman of power."

My hand reached instinctively for the Stone of Blood pendant hanging around my neck—the Balefire family heirloom. Giving it to me had been the one nice thing my mother had done for me my entire life unless you count getting banished to a nexus for twenty-five years and leaving me with my faerie godmother and her sisters as nice—and in my book, it definitely counted.

"I thought we only used our talismans for Awakenings?"

Mine had been the one piece of the puzzle I'd lacked, causing a decade-long delay in awakening my witch powers. Sylvana's motives for giving it to me hadn't been entirely pure—I didn't think she had an altruistic bone in her body—but even considering what I'd endured since, I was grateful she'd made an effort.

"Apparently not, and I'm afraid to ask my mother where she keeps it. She's not too happy with me for going to your grandmother for help. Even less so because the baby is related to you. No offense."

"None taken." I lied.

"If I saw what she did with it after my Awakening, I don't remember, and even if I did have the guts to call and ask, she probably wouldn't answer the phone. She's at some symposium or retreat in the Andes, and I have no idea when she'll be back."

"You're all alone? Are you sure you don't want to come stay with us?" I'd already asked Serena a half dozen times if she would be more comfortable with friendly witches around, and I doubted her answer would be any different this time.

"About two seconds after Ma left, Daddy got a call for a big, out-of-town job. To be honest, I'm enjoying the peace and quiet, aside from obsessing about the labor. But I still can't believe I gave up my apartment. Now I'm stuck here for who knows how long."

"You haven't heard from…"

"Jett? No. And I hope I don't. The less he knows

about the baby, the better."

I totally agreed but before I had a chance to answer, someone banged on the front door like a hammer on a nail.

"Serena, let me in."

Speak of the devil, and he appears. Not that my half-brother was on the same level as the ruler of the underworld. Not even close, though you couldn't tell it from the way Jett postured. You've probably heard the term delusions of grandeur, but Jett suffered from delusions of villainy.

A haunted look on her face, Serena called out, "Go away, you jerk. I don't want to see you."

He pounded again. "Let me in, Serena. I need to talk to you."

"You don't have to open the door. Do you want me to get rid of him?" Yeah, I butted in. Sue me.

Not that my talking to him would be any more effective than peeing on a forest fire, given our brief history. Jett would never forgive me for committing the grave sin of existing. Like it was my choice or something.

Or for Flix banishing him to the Faelands for his part in Kin's near demise the day we retrieved the Bow of Destiny from my grandmother's hiding place. If he was waiting for an apology from me, it would come about three days after they held the winter Olympics in hell.

"No, but I'm glad you're here." A sentence I think neither of us ever expected Serena to utter.

"I'll just go in the other room so you can have a little privacy. Call if you need me."

Serena squared her shoulders, straightened her spine, and moved toward the door. The look she threw over her shoulder held the fire of a she-bear protecting her young.

"Go get him," I murmured as I rounded the corner and positioned myself to eavesdrop from the hallway without a shred of shame. I told you I had stalker tendencies.

A sharp creak announced the door swinging open with some force.

"What do you want?" Serena practically growled.

"Nice greeting after all I've been through. Come on, baby, aren't you glad to see me?" I heard the shuffling of feet which I imagined was Serena taking herself out of arm's reach. "You look good, doll. A little soft around the edges, but the extra weight works on you. Just makes you more luscious."

Oily scumbag. One consolation: he didn't trip for me as Serena's soul mate.

"Nice try, Jett. I know you've been back for ages, so if you think you can show up now and I'll fall all over you, it's not happening."

I chanced a peek around the corner and saw Serena angling her body away to keep the burgeoning baby bump from showing as she settled back into her spot at the table. His back to me, Jett took the adjacent seat and tried to capture her hand. Over his shoulder, her gaze met mine and she treated me to a small smirk.

"Who told you that? The pitiful excuse of a Fae halfling who sent me on a trip to hell?" Jett scoffed. "That's always been your problem, Reen. You're so gullible."

Arrogant moron didn't feel the mounting power of Serena's fury?

"Not anymore, Jett. You'd be surprised the way things have changed while you were gone."

Confident he could get around her show of rejection, Jett brushed off Serena's assurance and launched into his reason for being there.

"Stupid Fae had no idea he was doing me a favor when he banished me to Faerie. I found a guy who knows someone who says she saw my father a few months ago. It's not a solid lead, but it's the best I've had in a long time. Will you help me find him? Once he's restored to power, Lexi will have to give up the bow, and he'll make me his right-hand man. You know I'll need you by my side. You're with me, Reen. Right?"

Jett's words struck a chord with me that I would rather have ignored.

Wishing for the chance to meet my dead mother featured high in my fantasies until it finally happened and the reality of her flaws set in. I'd feel sorry for Jett if he hadn't done everything in his power to try and keep me from finding the Bow of Destiny and using it for its intended purpose. Somewhere in his twisted mind, Jett thought tipping the scales of cosmic balance toward lovelessness would force our father out of wherever it was he'd taken himself off to for the past twenty-odd years—if only to fix the situation.

Since my work planted me firmly in the *love conquers all* camp, we were pitted against each other.

Typical abandoned child, seeking attention from the one source unavailable to provide it. Positive or negative in nature mattered little; it was all the same to Jett, who fit into every negative male stereotype in existence. He was possessive, controlling, selfish, and egotistical enough to make Narcissus blanch. Who cared if dear old Dad ever did show up and was disappointed? At least Jett would be the center of his focus, no matter what the consequences.

Tip the scales…the phrase triggered my memory. Of course, why hadn't I put the pieces together before? That opposing force I'd felt in the alley yesterday must have been Jett. It hadn't *felt* like Jett; had contained more power than I thought him capable of wielding, but who else could it be?

"Like I said, things have changed. Lexi!" Serena called my name, and I stepped into the room.

In an act of satisfying pettiness, I cuffed my half-brother on the back of the head as I passed by him to take a seat where I had a good view of his shocked face. Still sporting the sharply-plucked eyebrows beneath a heart-shaped scar and Mephistophelian goatee, he looked no worse for his unplanned vacation to the world of Faerie—in fact, the trip seemed to have fortified him somehow.

Enough to account for a major power boost? Maybe.

It would be colossally stupid to use Fae magic against a witch with at least three faerie godmothers at her disposal. Typical Jett. I made a quick mental note to pick said godmothers' brains for more information and fixed my brother with my most withering stare.

"Interesting company you're keeping these days." Jett's voice turned cool.

"If by *interesting* you mean infinitely better than a half-witted slug, you'd be right."

"Come on, Sis, I thought you'd be happy to see me safe and sound. I'd think you would want to find our father just as much as I do. We're family after all." Jett puffed out his chest in an attempt to look intimidating, but there was tension in his shoulders, a stiffness to his stance. He rolled the word family around on his tongue, then spit it out as though it tasted like a bitter pill.

Jett and I shared a father, plenty of bad blood, and nothing else that resembled what I considered to be a proper family tie. Cupid loved the ladies, given his reputation for spreading himself over a wide area. How many half-siblings might be waiting to pop out of the woodwork was a question I dared not take a guess at answering. So far, Jett had been the only one to come forward. Maybe they all blamed me for our father's love-'em-and-leave-'em philosophy. Cheerful thought.

Still, I could have cheered when Serena put him in his place.

"Go take your daddy issues out on someone who cares—a good therapist, maybe. Better yet, try that psychiatrist with the TV show. You'd probably get a discount rate for airing your angst to the world, and if you're lucky, you'll find some other fool gullible enough to take up with you, because I'm done."

Jett gaped at Serena in disbelief and shook his head, "You're going to regret getting involved with her, mark my words." It might have been the first time she had ever stood up to him, and the sadistic control freak had no idea how to take it.

"I could say the same about you," I answered for Serena, who leaned back in her chair, rested one arm nonchalantly on the table, and fixed her ex with a smirk. "Oh, wait, she already did. I believe my friend asked you to leave, big brother. Why don't you do as she says before we decide to hex you six ways to Sunday."

Mouth rounded like a fish at feeding time, Jett glanced back and forth between us for a few seconds. I figure he was trying to remember if he'd said anything I could use against him, but got caught up in the attempt to form words around the shock of seeing me with Serena.

"You wouldn't…"

"Try me." I rose and pulled out my wand, heard the rustle of clothing as Serena did the same. "No, really. I mean it."

"I'm…" Jett couldn't seem to find words and, rightly so, decided he was outnumbered. He pushed back his chair and headed toward the door.

"And don't come back," Serena called out with finality.

When the door closed behind him, she swallowed hard and burst into tears.

"I don't know why I'm crying like this. It must be hormones or something."

I sighed and asked a question I wasn't sure I wanted to be answered. "Do you love him?"

"No. Yes. No. Maybe. I don't know. I loved the way he made me feel important and needed. He told me I was powerful. Now I think he just played on those emotions to keep me in line. But I *am* going to have his baby, and he doesn't even know it. I should have told him, right?"

That was the million dollar question. What would Jett do if he found out Serena was carrying his child? Probably nothing good.

"If you really believed that, you would have already told him about the pregnancy. Trust your instincts, Serena. It's usually the best course of action."

"Maybe you're right."

If my calculations were correct, their baby would be one-quarter god and half witch—witch blood trumps human when it comes down through the mother's side—enough of both, I was almost certain, to create a Fate Weaver. Jett knowing that piece of information would be like Pandora's box and a can of worms opening at roughly the same time and with explosive force.

"How much did Jett tell you about me and our—parental situation? Besides us being half-siblings, I mean." I didn't want to mention the term Fate Weaver to her in case she knew something and hadn't yet put the pieces together, or worse, had no idea and wanted me to explain it to her. I didn't know enough about Fate Weavers to be a credible source of information, even though I was one. How ridiculous is that?

Serena opened her mouth to speak, and then the implications set in, and she looked like someone hit her with a stick. The tears started up again.

"I never thought...I've been so stupid. My baby will be the granddaughter or grandson of Cupid, and I'm a witch. That means I'm carrying a potential Fate Weaver. No wonder Clara's been looking at me like I have two heads and only half a brain sometimes. Some of the stuff she said makes more sense to me now."

Ah, so Serena *had* been paying attention, though

apparently she'd only focused on the demigod aspect and ignored the bigger picture. "I wish I had an inkling of what that means under normal circumstances, but unfortunately, I don't. I'm guessing my experience would have been entirely different had I Awakened my witch powers at the normal time. What I do know is that both sides of my heritage work together in a unique way—and it's heightened for me due to the Balefire bloodline."

Pointing out the differences in our heritage sounded like a slur, but I didn't mean it that way.

"Too bad they don't make a *What To Expect When You're Expecting - Fate Weaver Edition.*"

"Yeah, no kidding. Bottom line, Serena, is that you have the support of the entire Balefire clan, faerie godmothers and all. Besides, I'm a Fate Weaver, and I turned out okay. Don't laugh."

Serena grinned from ear to ear, "Yeah, you're not so bad. Sometimes."

Chapter 3

They say home is where your heart is, and while so cliché it makes me cringe, the phrase is one hundred percent truth. My house on the outskirts of the quaint coastal city of Port Harbor had been crowded when it was just me and my four faerie godmothers living there.

Now, the place was packed to the gills with the addition of my returned-from-the-dead grandmother, Clara; her Raythe-hunter-extraordinaire sister, Mag; and three familiars who shapeshifted between human and cat form, requesting large amounts of salmon at the drop of a hat.

Still, as I approached the driveway and tuned up my witch senses to pierce the veil of magic that—in theory— kept the neighbors' prying eyes and ears from taking note of all the weird goings-on, a gentle hum of activity from inside helped calm my jangled nerves. For once, I wasn't dreading an impending disaster on the other side of the front door. Mainly because my grandmother had a firm hand on the chaos and would not hesitate to put the faeries into her patented brand of time-out if they started a fracas about nothing—their favorite kind.

The household had begun to find its natural rhythm and at least a temporary sense of harmony. It helps when everyone has played a role in saving everyone else's lives a time or two. And when my fourth godmother was spending most of her time with her demon boyfriend. Don't get me started on that one, though.

Peace and tranquility. Two things I didn't trust to last, but I planned to enjoy the precarious balance for as long as possible.

"Rat bastard completely stomped what was left of my cottage right into the ground!" Mag thundered around the kitchen table with her fists in the air, the hem of her mustard yellow batik skirt rustling at her feet. I wondered if the offending garment was a relic from the 1970's, stowed away in some buried trunk full of fashion faux-pas from years past.

Dropping my bag on the table, I plunked down a stool at the breakfast bar and prepared to get the scoop. "Who did?"

"Stupid giant. Goes by the name of Bert. He's supposed to stay on his side of the mountain, but since I haven't been around to keep him at bay, he decided to squat in my house. Literally. On my house."

"Can't you guys help with that?" I turned my attention to four unusually silent faeries who avoided my gaze. "Well?"

"It's not that simple in the Fringe. Technically, we're not allowed to perform magic there." Terra replied.

"It's fine for everybody else, though. Seers and readers and witches make mistakes, too, but they all get a pass." Vaeta snapped. Her temper, though, showed itself in the extra force she used on the bowl of whatever she was whipping up. Froth arced up out of the stainless steel and threatened to plaster itself all over the counter, but she whiffed it back into the bowl with a flick of a finger.

There was a story there, but I didn't want to distract from Mag's problem, so I'd ask for details later. "There's a difference between turning cards and rearranging the elements whenever it strikes your fancy. And you do have a reputation for being cantankerous."

"We'd get ejected and banned for the next ten years. But we'll take the hit if you want us to," Fire faerie, Soleil, turned from the stove and offered with more excitement than I felt necessary. Raising a ruckus seemed to appeal to her, but why not? Soleil's temperament matched her element.

"No, that's not the answer," Mag said loudly. "And I won't have you getting into hot water on my account. I'll just find another place." She patted fuzzy strands of age-whitened hair back into place but kept the sour look on her wrinkled face. Battling Raythes had cost aunt Mag her youthful appearance. One of the perks of being a witch is that we age slowly and live extraordinarily long lives. While my grandmother, Clara, counted her years in centuries, she could have been mistaken for my older sister. In reality, Margaret and Clara were less than a decade apart, but you would never know it to look at them.

I could sense the frustration in her tone and theorized that although she loved being part of the family, solitude was Mag's default and she liked it that way. But there's always a third option.

"Why don't we just build another addition on the house?" I looked to Gran, who had maintained her silence up till now, for confirmation.

"Unless we decide to take up that…" Mag began a sentence.

"It's one option. I like us all being together, but I do agree we can't continue living like sardines in a can." Gran quelled her sister with a look, and I wondered what was going on with them.

But since they were offering me their best innocent faces, I let that go as well. "You keep talking about stinky little fish, and the familiars will demand a case of them. I can't stand sardine breath."

Gran smiled, but I could see doubt lurking behind her eyes. I guessed it had more to do with whether the faeries could make it through another remodel without scratching one another's eyes out. She had laughed like a lunatic when I regaled her with tales from the last time, but it's easy to find humor in someone else's miserable experiences and less simple when you're the one who has to deal with the fallout.

The more I thought about it, the more I liked the idea of an expansion. There was plenty of room in the backyard what with Terra's influence turning a postage stamp sized lot into acreage. "This is going to require a family meeting. Salem, go summon Pye and Jinx, and we'll get started making a list of everyone's suggestions."

"It's going to take more than a family meeting." My familiar's dark words matched his ebony skin. He raised the eyebrow over his green eye and scowled with the blue one. "And why bother with Jinx? Lazy so-and-so never comes out of cat form, and does nothing but hog my favorite sunny spot all day."

Salem preferred to be the top familiar in the house, and with both Gran's and Aunt Mag's hanging around he felt his position slipping.

"Be nice, and stop being such a worrywart. We survived the last remodel." My mind tacked a *barely* onto the end of the sentence, but I managed not to let it slip out. Salem was winning our ongoing game of "I told you so" by about 2-1, and if I didn't engage at least I could cite plausible deniability later. Truth be told, he was probably right.

I rolled my eyes and raced up to my bedroom to change in case things got messy. On the way, I checked my phone for about the millionth time. No new messages from Kin. I punched in his number and hit "send," not quite sure what I'd actually say when he answered. Two and a half rings and I got shuffled off to voicemail. Did my boyfriend just ignore my call?

I declined to leave a message, and instead jabbed at the "end" button and threw the offending device onto my bed.

Probably working and couldn't pick up—sounded like an excuse rather than a reason, but my philosophy of letting things go today would not be derailed. Changed, I headed back downstairs.

"Twinkleberry wine or coffee?" Terra raised a perfectly-groomed eyebrow and tossed me a sly grin. Eyes the color and texture of pink granite sparked with mischief. As much as she liked to consider herself a mother figure—or would that be an earth mother figure since that is her element?—she enjoyed jumping into the fray just as much as the rest of them. The same soil that she could coax into producing a tropical plant in the dead of winter could become a powerful weapon in her hands. Still, she made the best wine. Magically potent wine. Best taken in small doses if one preferred to retain any sense of decorum.

"Both would be wise." If I didn't want to end up

dancing naked in the backyard and blacking out for an entire day, that is. "Maybe half a glass of wine for me."

Carrying a large book under her arm, Soleil bustled back into the kitchen just in time to nod in agreement.

"This is my favorite book of house designs. It has some great ideas in it, and the pictures are simply marvelous."

We all settled around the dining room table with glasses of wine. I took a swig for fortitude and sat back to watch the fireworks show. Bottoms up.

Elemental and temperamental are more than just rhyming words in my house. They're descriptions for the four faerie godmothers who stepped in to care for me when a magical mishap during an epic feud landed my mother in a portal prison cage, and my grandmother in the clearing across the street—turned to stone for nearly a quarter of a century. Now that I thought about it, there were plenty of volatile tempers to go around.

I'd lost track of the number of faerie fights I'd been called on to referee over the years, but I know the signs like the back of my hand. First, the opening insult, followed by great offense being taken, then the name calling phase. If you catch them at that point, it's easier to diffuse a fight. Once the opening volley of magic gets thrown, it's better to let them go at it for a little while—releases the pressure—and then you can come in and lower the heat.

Faerie godmothers are to witches what guardian

angels are to humans. Under normal conditions, a witch never gets the opportunity to meet his or her godmother—or godfather if those exist, I've never asked—but my conditions had never been normal. Terra, the Fae assigned to me, took over my care when I was left a virtual orphan. She had drawn in two of her sisters, Evian and Soleil, to help with the task.

The fourth sister, Vaeta, had only joined us recently. Before that she'd committed the grave sin of following her boyfriend, Rhys, to the underworld where she was trapped—or chose to stay, we're all a little fuzzy on the details—for a hundred years.

I'd grown up with three women of such rare beauty that it fairly swept the breath away to look at them—until they were fighting, and then the pretty took a turn for the scary sometimes. Like now.

Something Soleil, faerie of fire, said caused great offense to water faerie Evian, which proved correct the adage about fire and water not mixing. Within seconds, they were in stand-off position. Soleil's short cap of flame-colored hair flicking around perfectly pale skin and her eyes kindling to embers, she rose fast enough to knock over her chair. A sheen of flame encased her body as she prepared to wield her element.

Polar opposite to her fiery sister, Evian juggled a ball of water between fingers tipped with mirrored nails, and surveyed her opponent with eyes the color of a whitecap wave. Evian's hair undulated as though floating on a gentle current—until she got riled up and the frenzy turned the current to a whirlpool.

"Ladies, please. There's no need for..." Terra's attempt at an intervention only served to turn the fury on her. Water and fire met earth in a scalding blaze of mist and mud. Vaeta, faerie of air, refused to be left out, and sent a strong breeze—okay, more like a mini tornado—toward Terra. I think her intention was to help, but all she managed to do was fling mud over most of the kitchen.

I saw the whole thing coming—this was not my first or hundredth time—grabbed my glass, and ducked under the table. From my position, I didn't get to see what happened next, but I heard my grandmother utter a sound somewhere between a snort and a sigh before a pregnant silence fell.

With nothing more than a few droplets of mud clinging to my clothes, and my wine glass relatively clean, I took a sip and waited. Patience can be a virtue in these situations, and Gran was certainly capable of diffusing the fight.

Frankly, it was a relief to have someone else play referee for a change.

Curiosity trumps patience, though, and after a final, fortifying sip, I poked my head out to see what was going on.

Four muddy faeries and two equally muddy witches engaged in a staring contest. Salem and the other familiars had been smart enough to revert to cat forms and scamper upstairs long before it got ugly.

If I'd been fully sober, I might have kept my mouth shut. "Mudslinging. The true sport of champions." It slipped out before I could stop myself.

Mud is good for the complexion, so at least I had that going for me, and for an hour or so, there'd been no time to obsess over the silence coming from my cell phone.

Chapter 4

Where was Vaeta and her magical hangover cure when I needed her? Not that I'd had enough wine to generate much of a buzz.

Between the upheaval at home, my encounter with Jett, and the Bow of Destiny conducting a never-ending symphony between my ears, I could actually see my temple throb with each beat of my heart. Pain led to tension, and now my neck and shoulder muscles boasted more knots than a sailboat.

Okay, maybe I did take one or two sips more wine than I should have, but Twinkleberry only bestows hangovers if you're already tense.

Gran said the rules aren't quite so stringent when it comes to casting healing spells on yourself, but I'd yet to achieve even the mending of a hangnail, had no patience for the mixing of herbs at the moment, and the crisp late autumn night air was calling to me anyway.

That's what it was—a sore back and shoulders—that roused me from sleep and sent me tooling the few blocks to the closest twenty-four-hour drug store at nearly two in the morning. Or maybe it was the Bow of Destiny, I don't know.

Either way, I cringed over each bump and around every corner until, by the time I parked Bluebell as close to the entrance as possible, my neck was so rigid I could barely look around. Perhaps that's why I didn't notice the classic black Corvette parked three spaces to my right.

Dismounting, I hobbled inside through a whoosh of artificial heat that contrasted so starkly with the cold night air I realized just how close we were to the time when I'd have to park my scooter for the winter. It seemed like only yesterday air conditioning had been the default setting. My life moved so quickly from one worrisome problem to the next lately, the passage of time had become somewhat arbitrary.

Even the rainbow rows of a thousand shades of nail polish couldn't distract me, and I beelined it for the first aid aisle after catching a glimpse of my mussed hair in one of those miniature funhouse mirrors next to the $5.99 sunglasses. Under normal circumstances, the sight of myself in such a state would have induced a mild panic attack followed by a minor glamour spell to spare the unsuspecting from the hideous sight of me, but I doubted the poor SOB working the night shift would even bat an eyelash at my appearance.

Whoever decided to place the sexual wellness section next to products designed to relieve aches and pains was either a genius or possessed a twisted sense of humor. I barely registered the canoodling couple browsing the display until the man spoke out loud and my heart dropped into the soles of my shoes.

I'd love to say I kept my cool and slowly turned around to unobtrusively glance at him, but when you're 99.9 percent sure you just heard your boyfriend say something scandalous to another woman, reason goes out the window along with poise and concern for whether you look like a crazy person or not.

"Kin?" My voice trembled so hard I loathed myself.

"Lexi. Hi." He had the good sense to at least look uncomfortable. "What are you doing here?"

"What am *I* doing here? *You're* supposed to be in Chicago for another two days." I slid my eyes over to his *companion* and nearly vomited.

Blond, perfectly blown out hair with golden highlights flowed around her lovely face, the tips resting on a bosom that practically burst out of the thin V-necked tee that skimmed the top of her navel. A sparkling pink belly button ring winked at me, and I resisted the urge to grab it and tug. Hard. Apparently, she hadn't read the memo that winter was coming, and it was now sweater weather.

Kin made no move to introduce me, and the woman's eyes flicked between us before she made up her mind and held one dainty, manicured hand toward me in greeting.

"I'm Rachel. Nice to meet you. Are you a friend of Kin's?"

I glared at her fingers with enough contempt to shrivel a grape into a raisin and shoved my hands into the pockets of my coffee-stained hoodie.

"No, I guess not." My world fell to pieces that littered the nondescript tiles, and no one noticed but me.

Shrugging, she smiled hesitantly up at Kin, who had the nerve to place his hand on the small of her back.

"I was going to call you." Kin's eyes were devoid of emotion, and upon the realization of that fact, I began to feel the insistent swell of magic from somewhere deep inside me. Not the kind that turns frogs into princes, either, or even the other way around. This was dark, wicked magic and had I allowed myself to hang around long enough to decide which one of the offending parties to target first, we might have had a ground-zero situation on our hands.

"Don't bother." I retorted, mustering up as much composure as I possibly could, turned on my heel and stalked back down the aisle. Adrenaline burned through the pain in my legs, and I broke into a run that had me out the door and straddling Bluebell before the tears began to flow.

And just like that, it was done. My heart was broken, and the man I'd imagined a future with was wrapped around a bleached-blond bimbo who could have been classified as my polar opposite.

There's not enough chocolate in the world to cure the kind of heartbreak that comes from being disconnected from your soul mate—and I knew Kin was mine. Magically fated, and until this minute, I'd never have doubted our destiny together.

He knew it too—or at least he had, once upon a time. Or six weeks ago. It suddenly seemed more like six years since we'd discussed moving in together and beginning our life. Bile bubbled up to replace the flavor of magic on my tongue, and I was barely able to stop the scooter before puking my guts out behind a bush at the end of my street.

Sweat glistening on my forehead and a foul taste in my mouth, I drove the rest of the way with a numb resignation that covered up a seething mass of desperate pain. How can you die inside and keep on living? That was the question of the night.

I stumbled back into the house expecting to slither up to my room and cry myself to sleep but instead walked into another Balefire family tradition: the midnight snack. Or, in this case, the 2:15 AM snack. Had it really only taken a total of twenty minutes for my love life to implode? Or had I been ignoring the signs that Kin and I weren't fated for each other after all?

Seven pairs of eyes widened as I spilled into the kitchen and began the process of melting down. Gran and Mag, still wearing their traveling cloaks, were knee deep into a half-gallon of butter pecan ice cream. The one tiny part of my brain not shrieking in pain wondered where they'd been at this time of night.

Salem crunched into a turkey and salmon sandwich (yuck), and all of the godmothers had slices of steaming pepperoni pizza in their hands.

"We thought you were upstairs sleeping. What's happened?" Gran asked, abandoning her spoon to wrap a protective arm around my waist. Terra rushed over to help me into a chair and brushed a stray lock of hair behind my ear in a gesture so filled with motherly love it pushed me over the edge.

"It's Kin," I blubbered, followed by a slew of unintelligible gobbledygook pouring out of my mouth. Thankfully, everyone in the room save for Salem spoke hot mess.

"What did that Mackintosh Clark do now?" He asked, his eyes narrowed in suspicion. I don't think he'd ever forgiven Kin for needing a minute to absorb the fact that I'm a witch and causing me a night of tearful sobs when we'd first begun dating. Or for kicking him out of his favorite kitty bed, the polka-dotted beanbag in my room while we were doing other things than sleeping.

Somehow knowing the cat also had manlike qualities gave Kin a case of the squicks.

"He's bought himself a one-way ticket to Hades, that's what he's done." Vaeta, who had the loosest lips in the bunch, shot back. "I know a nice, dingy nexus we can plop him into." Of all the faeries, you might expect the fiery Soleil to be the most ruthless when it came to exacting revenge against an enemy, but airy faerie Vaeta had a mile-wide ornery streak. And Kin had just made the top of her list.

If I hadn't been so full of my own despair, it would have made me smile to know the newest member of the godmother staff cared enough to want to protect me. Was I wicked for contemplating the offer? Or was I just the same as any of the other scorned women who'd been exacting their revenge for centuries? Hurt beyond repair and searching desperately for peace.

"That's too easy," Terra spoke through gritted teeth. "I'll blast him to the nether regions of the Faelands if you'd prefer never to see him again."

"Now, ladies, there are a million places we could send the boy; but that won't teach him a lesson. I know a good shrinking spell that'll shrivel his chances of pleasing another woman for the rest of his life. That's justice." Mag's eyes sparkled at the thought.

Everyone, even Gran, offered suggestions, each one worse than the last, for what sort of punishment to exact upon the man for hurting me. By the time we were done he'd been maimed and cursed a hundred different ways, and I hadn't been able to hold back a grin at the thought of him actually sporting a butt for a head.

"You all know we can't do any of those things, right?" I had to say it, or who knows in what state Kin might wake up tomorrow morning. A case of pus-secreting warts would certainly let him know he messed with the wrong family of witches, but I knew it wouldn't truly make me feel any better about the situation and the resulting backhand slap for using that kind of magic wouldn't be worth the price. Probably.

Ask Tommy Walker, who slapped me across the face in ninth grade, how it felt to be on the receiving end of one of the godmothers' whammies. Though, to be fair, he probably had no clue I had anything to do with him walking around looking like a Garbage Pail Kid for three days. Tommy had only been fifteen; I couldn't fathom what they were capable of inflicting on a grown man.

"Of course, dear." Gran answered for the group, "But imagining his demise is part of the healing process. And if you two work things out, we'll never speak of this conversation again."

"I don't think we're going to work it out, Gran. He's seeing someone else. And he's probably thrilled not to have to deal with my brand of crazy anymore."

Her response included a shrug and a shifty eye, "It never seemed like he minded before."

Kin never *had* seemed to care that I was different, save for his initial reaction the night I'd revealed I was a witch. I hadn't known my father's identity at the time, nor had I ever even heard the term Fate Weaver. Kin had weathered each storm right along with me—sometimes afraid I'd be harmed during one of my misadventures, but always supportive.

He'd embraced the fact that I was raised by four faeries, and didn't so much as bat an eyelash when he found out my grandmother was frozen in stone across the street from my house. Heck, the man had dealt with Salem sneaking back into the room and finding his often skyclad form sleeping at the foot of our bed with more understanding than he probably should have.

Perhaps he'd used up all his patience, and the break from our relationship felt like a breath of fresh air. Unfortunately, it didn't look like I was going to get the answers to any of my questions; Kin hadn't even bothered to tell me he was breaking up with me.

Red fury began to flare in the pit of my stomach, rising up to burn away the head and muscle aches, and tinging my cheeks a deep shade of crimson. It must have looked like my head was about to explode because Pyewacket's eyes widened to the size of saucers and she exchanged a concerned look with my familiar.

"Let it out, Lexi. Or you'll have bigger problems on your hands. You've scarce learned to control your power, and I've seen what a broken heart can do to a regular witch." Salem wagged a nagging finger in my face. "You remember what I told you about my previous charges, don't you? At least one of them was a woman scorned, and it didn't turn out well."

"You never said *how* she blew herself up! Maybe that should have been part of my briefing packet. Oh, wait, I never got one. Just a reaming for not having Awakened sooner and a metaphorical slap on the wrist." I knew he'd had bad luck with the witches before me, and was reluctant to elaborate on the specifics. Salem was currently living out his ninth and final life; after me, he wouldn't come back to serve another witch and loved to remind me that his length of time on this planet was inextricably linked with my own.

"There you go, that's much better." Leave it to Salem to poke a pin in the bubble of my wicked magic. If I hadn't been completely overwhelmed, I would have thanked him.

After that, the room began to feel much smaller than it ever had before, and I extracted myself with as little fanfare as possible and retreated to my rooms on the second floor.

Everywhere I looked there were reminders of Kin: our smiling faces pressed together in the framed photos on my dresser; his sweatshirt slung over my vanity chair; the memories of us snuggled together in my bed watching Netflix on Saturday afternoons. All painful, gut-wrenching blows to my heart and my ego.

I'd never shared as much of myself with anyone as I had with Kin, and I could feel myself toppling on the edge of self-destruction. I could either sit around wondering what was wrong with *me*, and be the kind of sad woman who pins all of her self-worth on a man, or I could look at the situation objectively.

Regardless of his reasons, Kin owed me more than an offhand breakup—in public, with his new girlfriend watching, no less—and it wasn't my fault he didn't man up and approach the situation with sensitivity and respect.

Well, fine. If that's how he wanted to play it, I'd make it even easier for him. No way was I going to do the walk of shame over to his place and let him watch me pack my things. If it was a clean break he wanted, that's what he was going to get.

I cast a net around my devastated heart, ignored its frantic struggles, and shoved that mess as far down into my emotional footlocker as it would go. Slamming the lid felt a lot like closing a coffin.

Chapter 5

Being repeatedly poked in the arm by someone trying to draw your attention is annoying enough, but when it happens in your head, it's beyond the pale. The Bow of Destiny lives inside me. Sort of, anyway, it's complicated. Half the time I'm thrilled to be the carrier of my father's weapon, the other half, I'm convinced it's some sort of parasite.

If there were any rhythm to the pattern for when I'd be called to its use, I'd yet to pick up on one. Who tells the bow when to make a match? I'd really like to know because I have a few questions. Like if I'm in the middle of lathering my hair, could it maybe wait a minute? Could I see the schedule ahead of time? I could plan things better with a little advance notice. I'd missed so many meals in the two months since becoming the bow's official wielder, I'd had to start carrying a bag full of snacks and energy drinks.

And then there was the mounting transportation problem. Scooting around on Bluebell, my new, but still vintage Vespa, in the winter? Ineffective and dangerous. Not all of my headaches are directly related to bow song blasting at odd times.

On the morning after Kin devastated me, I welcomed the distraction and followed the Bow's call without grumbling overly much. Maybe burying myself in Fate Weaver work would also bury the pain under a mountain of good deeds and that would be enough to keep me from falling apart.

Yeah, I was deluded. Cut me a break; sometimes you do what you have to in order to deal.

Besides, using Kin as an excuse was just that: an excuse. The whole truth was the need to ply my trade was as strong as the need to breathe and would not go ignored. Somewhere there was a couple in need, and I was the woman meant to help them.

That I was wearing polka-dotted pajama pants, winter boots, a ratty sweatshirt under a fur-lined hoodie and hadn't combed my hair went unnoticed by me, though not by people on the street. My feet seemed to know the way, and I fell into a daze as they carried me forward.

Or maybe into a Fate Weaver dream state.

It's entirely possible to feel both inconsequential and grandly important at the same time. Not healthy, mind you, but possible. No domino in a standing row is any more important than another until one falls and the whole dynamic changes. I needed to be the catalyst for fate or the hand that chooses which domino to tip and when to create the proper pattern.

If that sounded arrogant, I didn't mean I thought I was in charge of the world or anything. Just for my little role in the grand design.

Love carries both darkness and light in equal measure—anyone who has ever been dumped would agree—which makes the human heart a critical pivot point in the balance between those two concepts. Turn the world toward hate, and we'll destroy ourselves as history has shown time and again. Humans weren't meant to live only in the light, either. Just as we need the light of day, we must have the restful dormancy that comes in the dark of night.

Some little part of me, the bit that wasn't caught up in contemplating the dual nature of the universe, hooted and jeered that I was no different from anyone else or Kin would still be in my life. I wanted to punch that part of me in the throat.

All inner conversation stopped when the bow twanged a warning note, and I blinked back to full awareness of my surroundings. More than full awareness, if I'm being technical. Lexi Balefire, romance Jedi, sensed a disturbance in the force.

Hate snaked its tendrils around the couple arguing in front of the window of the bakery where my friend

Mona worked, and I felt like an alien as I stood there and watched. I didn't need to hear the content to know the words formed bitter and pointed missiles intended to wound. My inner Fate Weaver could see them as plain as day.

She could also see the light inside her intended targets. To her, it looked like a bird fluttering against the cage of darkness closing in around it, and she knew she must act before it was too late.

I don't remember calling the bow carrier, she was just there, arrow fitted to string, arm cocked and taking aim almost before she was fully released from my skin.

Yes. Yes. Do it. I mimicked her motions without thinking what that might look like to passersby. At that point, I barely remembered I had a body, much less any concern for what it was doing. All that existed was the need to fix this. The compulsion took me over. Dragged me under until the arrow sliced the hissing darkness, pierced hearts, and laid the matter to rest.

Anger rolled over me from the outside in. Someone out there was well and truly pissed off. Without taking time to think about it, I cast the leather-clad Goddess in the direction of the blackest emotion I'd ever felt turned my way. Pink-tipped hair flying, she tossed a surprised glance over her shoulder and surrendered her will to mine. It only lasted a matter of seconds before she was back, shaking her head to indicate failure, and then we were one again.

The fight over, I watched the happy couple light up the area around them with joy as they strolled into the bakery. Love spreads love. If you don't believe another word of my story, believe that.

Watching through the window while Mona bagged up their pastries, I wondered who might hate the young couple enough to use magic to try and tear them apart. At least this fix-it shooting had been sanctioned. My last attempt at a bow-induced reconciliation had gone all kinds of wrong when I forced the shooter to do my bidding. Lesson learned.

This, with outside forces acting on the couple, was a different scenario. Was it personal, and if it was, personal to whom? Me or the fighting couple.

Watching the couple flip from hate to love reminded me of the board game Othello. A simple game with one goal, to dominate the board by surrounding your opponent's pieces and flipping them, so their color matches your own. When the playing field is filled, the one with the most tiles showing their color wins.

What? You were expecting something more profound? In my house, board games are kind of a big deal.

On the cosmic side of things, I'd like to think I'm on the white team because while I do love the color black on a cocktail dress, when it comes to love, black and white carry stereotypical associations to good and evil. Love has to be good, right?

Maybe not.

Love, in and of itself, is neither dark nor light. It's just a playing piece waiting to be placed on the board and can be flipped like any other. My job is to make sure there are more white pieces in play than black. Feels a lot like whistling in the dark sometimes—mostly because I'm never sure who I'm playing against. That's another question I'd ask if I ever got the chance.

Right now, the simplest answer came down to the person who seemed to hate me the most. My brother, Jett Striker.

Chapter 6

My love life circling the toilet gave me no excuse for shirking work, and the idea of Jett mounting an assault on my clients demanded I make an appearance at the office and at least attempt to hold down the fort. I had a backlog of happy couple photos to post to the company website Flix had set up. Without my asking, mind you. I didn't bother with breakfast, figuring staring at lovey-dovey faces all day would probably give me indigestion anyway.

Flix had my best intentions at heart, and if the website garnered even a handful of clients, it would be worth the trouble. I was determined to keep up with my business even if I had a sideline job now. How odd was it that I moonlighted on myself?

Did I mention I hated technology? Or to be more specific, I hated anything computer-related. Flix probably knew a trick to upload the whole folder of images to the website in one fell swoop while I would have to slog away all day to get the same results.

What I really wanted to do was find my brother and clobber him over the head with a very large stick, but I'd learned that biding my time when it came to Jett Striker was usually the best course of action. Better to outsmart him; catch him off guard and really put the screws in. Though I was making a valiant attempt at stoicism, I lacked the energy to pursue Jett with any kind of gusto anyway. Patience is a virtue, but it doesn't count if avoidance and laziness are contributing factors.

"Girl, what are you wearing?" Flix strolled through the connecting door between our respective areas and pulled me out of my reverie. "Tell me you're not meeting clients like that."

"What? I'm fine." The defense was a reflex since I couldn't remember what I'd thrown on when I crawled out of bed.

"Fine? No. Nope. Not even close." Flix practically dragged me into the closet full of clothes donated by local shops for advertising purposes. Days like these, I was glad my matchmaking abilities had a wider scope than simply putting dewy-eyed couples together. If FootSwept went under, at least I'd have a way to pay the bills.

The woman staring back at me from the slick, full-length mirror was an absolute mess. Hair in tangles, makeup styled by a raccoon, and bunny slippers. I'd walked to town in my jammies. What a horror show.

That Flix had been working hard to curb his empathic reaction showed when he had to ask what had happened to me to cause such a meltdown. His reaction was unsatisfyingly neutral and I had to wonder if he still harbored a grudge over our recent disagreement.

But then, I remembered he'd become friends with Kin and wouldn't be indulging in a round of verbal flogging of my ex. And so, without taking sides or asking my permission, something he'd never do under normal circumstances, Flix used magic to re-clothe me and style my hair. Nothing, not even magic, could completely erase the haunted look in my eyes, but at least I was presentable.

"Thanks, I…thanks. Between Kin, the state of affairs at FootSwept, and the return of our very favorite meddling Son of Cupid, well…things aren't exactly kosher."

"You'll get through this." Flix gives the best hugs. Maybe it's his magically enhanced empathy or something in his Fae heritage, but when his arms come around you, there's a feeling of safety and light. "Kin will come to his senses; our clients will come back around once they figure out they were better off with Lexi Balefire on their side; and as for your brother," Flix's eyes narrowed to slits, and I saw a glimmer of the formidable Fae show through, "He will regret whatever soul-sacrificing deal he had to make to escape the

Faelands."

"That would have required him to possess a soul worth trading in the first place. I've been wondering how he managed it, and I had hoped his little trip would be enough to deter him from messing with us. Once again, I've underestimated his stupidity."

Funneling annoyance into useful pursuits, I tidied up the closet while Flix leaned against the door frame and watched. Our long history had taught him never to get in my way when I went on a cleaning binge, but he listened to the tale of my encounters with dark energy, giving me his full attention. Halfway through, I was interrupted by the bell that signaled a client had come through the main entrance.

Hoping the smile on my face looked natural and not reflective of how I really felt, I stepped through the connecting door and stopped in my tracks when I saw the woman standing in my office.

I recognized her right away, how could I not? The way her face was splashed all over town.

"Lexi, right? It's nice to finally meet you, I'm Diana Diamond."

A red power suit skimmed and molded over lush curves and somehow struck the perfect balance between *caring broker of love* and *no-nonsense businesswoman*. I could see how easy it would be for clients to trust this woman on sight. I didn't, but then I've learned the hard way lately that people are not always what they seem.

Or maybe she was, and I just disliked her for horning in on my turf. I was entitled to be petty about my life's work.

She held out a hand, fingertips painted to match her suit, and I hesitated for only a fraction of a second before making contact.

I don't know what I expected to happen, but nothing did. Her hand felt remarkably normal. No jolt, no tingle. It pained me that I couldn't ask what brand of lotion she used to make her skin so soft, but I'd never in a million years admit to even the tiniest weakness, so I stuck to exchanging pleasantries while wondering what she wanted.

"You're my idol, you know," Diana continued. "The way you put couples together without relying on any sort of modern methods or technology. It's remarkable how your little business seems to work. I've been watching you for months. Your success rate is stellar."

Okay, now that was weird. How could she know anything about my success rate? I don't advertise, I don't post stats on a website, or a blog. I don't crow about my accomplishments. Had she been contacting former clients? Spying on me? And don't think I missed the slightly condescending use of the word "little" because I definitely caught it.

"Umm. Thanks." You creepy woman. I left that part off. "I'm not much for being in the spotlight. It's all about the matches." I hadn't meant it as a subtle dig. Or if I did, it came from somewhere in my subconscious.

"Of course, my clients' relationships come first; my methods are simply more lucrative than yours."

Flix fixed her with the kind of assessing gaze that was as revealing as an x-ray. What he said next would be meant to give me his opinion of her, and I paid attention.

"When greed feeds ambition, it's a dangerous combination; we prefer to supplement ours with generosity."

Diana's face changed. The mask of politeness fell away to reveal a cool, hard surface underneath. Her idol? My patootie. She'd come here to throw down some kind of gauntlet, though I wasn't sure what kind or why. I hadn't been garnering enough business lately to qualify as a rival.

"You couldn't imagine what motivates my ambition. I came here to let you know there's no animosity; business is business. I just wanted to meet the illustrious Lexi Balefire for myself, get a peek behind the curtain, as it were." With that, Diana Diamond scanned my office, tilted her nose up slightly, nodded once in my direction, and threw a red and white square of paper on my desk before taking her leave.

"What the heck was that all about?" I frowned at Flix and picked up the offending piece of paper—a business card styled to resemble a playing card, but with

Diana's phone number and email address printed across the back.

"Don't worry, that skanky wannabe will crawl back into her hole when she figures out she can't out-Lexi *the* Lexi Balefire. She might call herself the queen of hearts, but you're the real deal." Part of me still wished he'd used that same fire when talking about Kin.

"I certainly hope so."

Now that we were alone again, I felt what little energy I had been holding onto deflate along with my spirits. The two clients I met with that afternoon received stellar service, but only because I could still see Diana Diamond's smug face smiling at me and refused to let the encounter negatively affect business.

She put a chink in my armor, though. One big enough that when the professional misery overtook me, it popped the locked box where I kept my private pain. Utter heartbreak flooded back and dragged me along in its undertow until I felt bruised and bloody.

"Go home and get some rest." Flix's look of pity was too much for me to bear, and for once I followed his advice without argument. As vehemently as I'd tried not to succumb to my emotions, a broken heart wants what it wants. It was time to wallow, whether I relished the idea or not.

Approximately three days and four pints of my

favorite faerie-conjured, discontinued flavor of Ben and Jerry's—Bovinity Divinity, white and milk chocolate swirl with little cow-shaped chunks of more white and milk chocolate—and countless boxes of tissues later, I hit the ignore button on my cell phone and sent yet another call to voicemail.

I groaned when I noticed the number of pending messages from Mona Katz, feeling zero remorse for the slight. Why does everyone think the answer to all of life's difficult situations is to talk about it? Talking doesn't fix everything, and it certainly wasn't going to make the hole in my chest any smaller. Picking at a wound only invites infection, tears away the ragged edges to make room for greater pain. No thank you.

My bedroom looked as though a garbage truck had upchucked all over it, and I'd intentionally blocked Terra's cleaning charms along with any noise from below. Heavy drapes pulled tight kept out even a sliver of sunlight, and to be honest I had no clue what time or even what day it was.

When you've spent the entirety of your life feeling abandoned by your family, those emotions tend to rear their ugly heads on a hair trigger. Yes, I'd been blessed with four faerie godmothers to replace the biological one I'd lost, but feeling loved doesn't always negate the pain of betrayal. Raw deal for the ones who do the loving and raising, but I'd like to think I've appropriately shown my gratitude. In the moment, though, since that's where my mind wanted to go, I concentrated on the hurtful absences in my life rather than the loving presences.

And back down the rabbit hole I fell, letting waves of despair at Kin's betrayal and abandonment roll over me in their oxymoronic symphony of gentle, coaxing swells and turbulent, crushing billows, fusing with the pieces of me that had been treading in those waters for years. Past, present, and my lost future came together to be mourned all at once, and the force of it dragged me through the dirt, ripped me apart at the seams for what felt like the 259,200th time in as many seconds.

Reason takes a back seat when you're in the throes of an all-out mental breakdown, and without a compass to guide you back to sanity, the process drags on for as long as you'll let it. Somewhere, deep inside me, the bow carrier stirred, and I could feel her irritation palpitating my nerves to the brink of insanity. I ignored it, and her.

The deluge of tears pinched my eyes closed until eventually I fell back to sleep on a crumpled bag of Reese's Pieces, fully covered by a thick down comforter that failed to do what its name promised considering it still smelled faintly of Kin's aftershave.

Dreams always have a way of manifesting your greatest hopes and fears, and sometimes they do so in the most painful way possible. Emotional exhaustion gave way to deep sleep, but the blessed blackness burst into technicolor as I rode the long, sturdy ash handle of a broom and streaked across the sky.

Somewhere down below, I could hear the tortured cry of a familiar voice—Kin's voice, I knew without knowing, in one of those split seconds where you realize you're dreaming, but you don't wake up. I wouldn't have, even if I wanted to, because Kin's pain was like a siren's song to me and I'd do anything to save him whether he loved me or not.

Dipping low, I felt the night wind in my hair and could see blades of grass dancing in the light of the full moon, though my dream eyes couldn't penetrate the darkened perimeter of the forest where Kin's cries echoed.

And then I was running through the trees, searching for what seemed like hours before stumbling into a clearing where I saw Kin, chained to a pyre of licking Balefire.

He called to me, screaming my name over and over. It sounded like a curse in my ears and stripped the metaphoric skin from my bones.

Balefire is my element. In the same way the godmothers command earth, air, fire, and water, I serve this sacred flame. Its heat heals me, feeds my magic in a symbiotic relationship. Why, then, was the Balefire burning my one true love to ash?

Stepping into the flame, I felt its fingers tickle harmlessly across my skin until my questing hand touched Kin's arm and agony took me over. Burning, empty, hollowed out. The fire consumed him. Racing against time, I ignored everything except the knots that held him captive, burrowed my fingers into their coils to loosen them enough to set him free. The more I tried, the tighter his bonds.

The rain of my tears hissed and healed him where they touched, but only for a moment and the burning began anew.

I woke up in a pool of tears and sweat, screaming into my magically soundproofed room. Realizing it doesn't matter if a falling tree makes a sound when there's nobody there to hear it, I bit off my sobs abruptly and headed for the bathroom.

The face I saw staring back at me from the mirror wasn't entirely unfamiliar; Kin's not the first man I've ever cried my eyes out over. When you can sense your boyfriend's true soul mate—and it isn't you—falling in love with the wrong man becomes at best an exercise in futility, and at worst self-torture of the heart.

Most of those exes moved on quickly, some with my help, whether they knew it or not. Others sent flowers, continued trying to woo me, eventually skewing so far toward needy I might not have dated them again even if they *had* been my soul mate.

Seeing Kin trapped in the Balefire—basically trapped in me and my crazy life—was a moment of clarity. Who could blame him for wanting someone who doesn't have to charter a private plane to haul their emotional baggage back and forth? He'd wanted out, and he found the perfect excuse—a tall blond the exact opposite of Lexi Balefire.

Chapter 7

"Lexi Balefire, this has gone on long enough." Gran burst into my bedroom with Salem at her heels.

"You're bogarting the beanbag chair, and I've hit my limit." He whined as if his favorite sleeping spot should be my biggest concern.

Gran flung the curtains open and flicked her finger at the ankle-deep mish mash, which then started to organize itself into piles of clean and dirty clothes, garbage, and assorted candies that had gone rogue and hidden beneath my bed covers. There was a Skittle stuck to my face, and I just didn't care.

"Today is Thanksgiving, and you're going to participate with the rest of the family. You know I love you to the moon and back, but you've wallowed long enough, and if you don't get out of that bed, there will be consequences." Gran's tone brooked no refusal, but she shot another pointed look at me for good measure before heading back downstairs. "I expect you clean, dressed, and in the kitchen peeling potatoes in no less than half an hour. Don't make me come back up here," she warned.

I glowered at the door after she left and heard her tinkling laugh from down the hall, "I saw that."

Lexi, let yourself feel the pain, everyone had said following the breakup—and now that I was allowing myself to fully delve, I was expected to get over it just like that. Damned if I did and damned if I didn't.

I'd never mention it to Gran, but the shower felt amazing, and I took my time relishing the hot water cascading over my skin, washing the residue from the last few days down the drain.

My face looked paler than usual, and my eyes were still a bit puffy from crying, but I was at least wearing a respectable outfit when I descended the stairs thirty minutes later. A flurry of sounds reverberated through my bedroom door, and I knew when I returned, all evidence of my funk would be gone.

One thing I have to say about living with a group of magical beings: holidays rock. It's perfectly acceptable—more like insisted upon, if you want to get technical about it—to go completely over-the-top when it comes to decorating. I think it took the faeries at least a decade of living with humans to understand that not all holidays were created equal. We've stopped celebrating George Washington's birthday with the same fanfare as

Christmas, but Thanksgiving was still a banner day in the Balefire household.

Aunt Mag was a bit perturbed that nearly all the old traditions had gone ignored, and she and Gran tried their best to weave some Paganism in with our unabashedly Americanized customs. A good compromise meant leaving the cardboard turkeys in their plastic, color-coded bins in favor of a plethora of gourds, corn stalks, and overflowing horns of plenty to highlight the end of the harvest season.

"You decorated without me. Where are the glittered pumpkins?" A tradition with no historical basis whatsoever, and one which elicited a scathing comment from Aunt Mag when several faerie-dust covered pumpkins magically appeared. Some things you have to fight for and the cheery rainbow sparkles lifted my spirits enough to wash the last dregs of the dream about Kin out of my head. There would be good food, and people I loved. Plenty of reasons for cheer.

The gingery scent of pumpkin spice teased my olfactory senses while I fingered a garland of real multi-colored leaves adorning the banister, and I was beyond thankful when Terra stepped into the hall to pop a tartlet into my mouth and hand me a cup of steaming coffee.

"Too much pumpkin?" She bit her lip in consternation. I'd never known Terra to question a culinary choice before. "My taste buds seem off today.

Of all days."

I'd also never heard any one of the godmothers mention feeling less than stellar about anything. Maybe Gran's presence was bringing out their insecure sides.

"No, it's perfect," I assured her through a mouthful of creamy pie. "Can't be too much pumpkin in a pumpkin tartlet. That would be an oxymoron." Or some other term that I couldn't dredge up.

Soleil was busy readying the bird, and I've got to say it looked rather odd to see a turkey stuffing itself. By the time she popped it into the oven, its skin was covered in a homemade herb butter, and the scent of freshly chopped onions, garlic, and parsnips mixed pleasantly with the sweetness of a half dozen pies cooling on the windowsills.

A knock at the door sent my heart scurrying up to my throat, and for a split second, I thought it must be Kin coming for Thanksgiving. Sometimes, when pain is still fresh, you forget about it for a moment and then experience every horrifying second all over again.

The doorbell chimed again, and it took everything inside me to swallow my tears and answer the door.

"Hi Serena, come on in." I had completely forgotten about Gran inviting her for dinner. "How are you feeling today?"

She blew by me and made a beeline for the foyer powder room, "Like someone's sitting on my bladder." The door slammed shut, and I felt my cheeks turn up into the first grin I'd been able to manage for days.

Who woulda thunk it? Serena Snodgrass was in my house, and I wasn't trying to blast her back through the front door. I only hoped Vaeta and the rest of the godmothers would feel the same way; they'd behave or incur Gran's wrath, but I wanted zero tension today.

"You're going to be civil to our guest, right?" I raised an eyebrow at the four of them, who kept right on cooking without even sparing me a glance.

"Of course, dear," Terra assured me lightly.

"As long as she behaves herself." I'd never forgotten the time Vaeta witnessed my first blocking charm, which left Serena covered in bubble gum. I was new to witchcraft then, give me a break. It was a spur-of-the-moment decision that saved me from a face full of boils. Serena had deserved to have them turned on her since she sent them out in the first place. The bubble gum was my personal touch.

"Please believe that I've changed," Serena had crept into the kitchen behind me and spoke in a low but steady voice, "I'm truly sorry for all the trouble I've caused. I hope you can forgive me."

One thing I can say about the godmothers is that though they can hold a grudge against each other for centuries, they're quite forgiving when they know someone is truly repentant.

Vaeta surveyed Serena for a moment, and after a meaningful look at each of her sisters softened her face into a smile. "She speaks the truth and everyone deserves a second chance, but ours is not the final word. That responsibility falls on Lexi, and if she's found it in her heart to forgive, so can we."

A hint of the old Serena sneaked out when she muttered, "Forgiveness goes both ways, you know. Give me a little credit for doing the same."

"Pumpkin tartlet?" I offered with a genuine smile. "It's like a little bite of heaven."

She smiled back. "Just one? I'm eating for two. What can I do to help?"

The brief moment of tension passed, and everyone bustled around preparing for the afternoon's feast. If, of course, you can call flicking a finger and encouraging the potatoes to peel themselves bustling. Not that I was complaining. Despite Gran's orders for me to help with the cooking, it's just not my thing.

"So, did you find the talisman you were looking for?" I asked Serena while she, sans magic, coaxed a ball of biscuit dough into a circle with a rolling pin.

Serena sighed, her mouth settling into a thin line. "No, not yet, and I've done at least a dozen locator spells and scoured the house, but still nothing. I did find a love letter from Donny Dixon stashed in my hope chest, and one of those furry electronic pets we used to carry everywhere in third grade, but I don't think a pink animatronic owl is going to help me out of this bind."

"Probably not. I remember those things. I begged

for one for Christmas, and by New Years, the thing just would not stop yapping, so I tried to flush it down the toilet. When that didn't work, I wrapped it in a towel and buried it in the backyard. I think I saw him flying around out there a couple of years ago during one of the faerie's epic game nights. Creepy. And completely not the point. Gran, what exactly does this demigod birth entail?"

Startled, Gran and Mag looked up guiltily from where they huddled in a corner around Gran's cell phone. She put it back in her pocket and took a seat next to Serena.

"Lot of factors." Gran mused. "It's best to be prepared for anything from a normal birth to one with potentially epic magical complications. We can't assume the child's power will remain dormant until Awakening; yours didn't. You were able to use your Cupid-bestowed gifts before you gained your full magic."

"You knew that when Lexi was born?" Serena fished for information.

"Not exactly." Clara glossed over something she didn't want to say outright, "There will be indications of the baby's strength and proclivities, but I can't tell you in what form until I see them. Meanwhile, the baby needs nourishment, and I think we're just about ready to eat."

"Good, because I'm famished. I swear the baby has the appetite of an elephant."

"More than normal? I've heard that the mother's body will nourish the child in her womb first, and the mother second. Is that what's happening here?" I asked.

"Yes, exactly. All babies require great amounts of energy to grow and thrive. Think how exhausting it must be for human women." Aunt Mag made a tsking sound. "At least you have hardy witch blood running through your veins."

"Witch blood," the main ingredient in creating a family talisman. Mingling the blood of all who have gone before makes for strong magic. "That's why you need her amulet or whatever for the birth, right?"

"Right. That pendant you're wearing carries the blood of all the Balefire women in history; Serena's talisman is the same. A material repository of the blood magic that has been passed down through the ages. When the baby is born, we'll perform a binding ceremony, strengthening the bond between mother and child, and the Snodgrass talisman will be the item of focus."

"If we ever find it," Serena muttered.

"There's plenty of time. Now, can we eat?"

Not to be too sappy about it, but despite feeling bruised and broken, my heart swelled as my family gathered around the table. All the bits and pieces of it. So what if Flix was missing this year; he'd been invited to dinner with Carl's family. The all-important "meet the parents" dinner, no less. Talk about adding stress to the holiday.

If any image of Kin tried to intrude, I blocked it out amid the four-way tussle between the familiars—Serena's Morana had joined the ranks—over the gizzard. Mag ended that with an engorgement charm that made the nasty thing big enough to satisfy them all. Jinx, in a shocking turn of events, turned both loquacious and eloquent in a bid to draw Morana's jealous attention away from Salem and Pyewacket.

Serena kicked my foot under the table and made googly eyes at me when he launched into a tale about his tail. It worked, though. By the end of dinner, Morana and Jinx looked like they were on their way to having a thing.

"This is the first time I've heard him utter more than two words at a time," I whispered to Gran who sat on my other side.

She winked at me. "Talking about tail does that to a guy."

Her dry response made me choke on a bit of stuffing, and I got a whack on the back for my efforts. Thankfully, it dislodged a particularly hairy mental image of Jinx and Morana, so everything worked out for the best.

"Isn't it gorgeous out? Fifty-five degrees on Thanksgiving—how often does that happen?" Serena stretched out beside me on a porch chair, snuggled up beneath a fuzzy, almost unnecessary blanket while I sipped wine and tried to fight a post-turkey nap.

I barely managed an agreeable "mm-hmm" when Salem pounced on me, this time only figuratively. "We're forming teams for a flag football game in the backyard, and you've been drafted. Change and meet me on the field."

At any other time, I might have been tempted to try and get out of playing, but today was Thanksgiving and football was expected. Suddenly, getting some aggression out in the form of physical exertion seemed like precisely the type of distraction I needed.

Speaking of distractions.

"What on earth are you wearing?" I snorted once I'd taken a good look at Salem.

"What? Isn't this what football players wear?" He looked down at a cropped nylon jersey and a pair of the shortest shorts in existence with an expression of bewilderment mixed with suspicion. I've seen him naked on more than one occasion, and this was far worse.

It was at least thirty seconds before I could breathe, and it didn't help that Serena was both laughing and yelling at him to stop making her have to pee again.

Another fit of giggles garbled my response, "You're trying to keep the other team from stealing the flag from your belt; not attempting to persuade them into stuffing singles underneath it. Is there a bachelorette party in the other room? Go ask Google a couple of questions before you settle on an outfit."

"I swear to Hades, I'm going to kill that little fur ball…" I heard Salem mutter as he flickered into his regular clothes. A white button-down contrasted starkly against his supple, ebony skin. One blue and one green eye peeked out beneath the shock of white hair that remained even in his fuzzy cat form.

Salem and Jinx, Aunt Mag's familiar, weren't getting along. I think it had something to do with Salem's newfound interest in Pyewacket. Or maybe, today, it had with Morana's previous interest in Salem. Either way, I got the impression our newest addition took great pleasure in irritating Salem. It's always the quiet ones, you know?

"Wait, whose team am I on?"

"You're with Mag, Terra, Vaeta, and Jinx."

"That means you've got Pye, Clara, Evian, and Soleil. Fire *and* water. That doesn't seem fair. Plus, I have Aunt Mag, and what about Morana?"

"She's playing referee, and I wouldn't count your dear old Auntie out quite yet, Lexi," Vaeta chose that moment to stride into the entryway, "Or underestimate the advantages of having an air faerie on your side."

Aunt Mag greeted me at the bottom of the stairs once I'd changed into a pair of sporty leggings and a light sweatshirt, her feet jammed into exactly the type of sneakers you'd expect an old woman to wear—orthopedic-looking behemoths with Velcro straps.

"I hear you doubt my skills on the field, and I suppose that means you never heard about my illustrious career with the Harbor Harpies."

"The what now?"

"Intramural witch football. Running back. And I've still got a few moves." With that, Aunt Mag moonwalked down the hallway with a mischievous grin on her deeply-lined face. Only a few years older than her sister, Mag spent her youth early, fighting enough evil that even a witch of her caliber hadn't come away unscathed. "I just hope you're up for the challenge, lazy bones."

For Hecate's sake, the woman walked with a cane most of the time. How was she doing that? A spell or was she just a big fat faker who only looked older than dirt?

I rolled my eyes, but I hadn't been quite as active as usual lately, and you could never call me a gym rat anyway. Don't get me wrong; I work out. I think I took a yoga class about six months ago. That counts, right? And I definitely make it a point to walk around Port Harbor instead of relying on taxis or my little blue scooter—at least in the summer months. When it's not too hot. Fortunately, I inherited the Balefire family genes, and they come with a high metabolism and curves

I don't think I could achieve if I had Jillian Michaels chained up in my basement.

When I say I got the Balefire family genes, I mean literally. They might as well be a pair of actual jeans—the kind you wear till they fall apart because they fit your body like a second skin. My grandmother, mother, and I all look almost exactly alike—flowing chestnut hair, thick eyelashes, and a heart-shaped face with full, crimson lips. I lucked out; that's for sure. And since witches don't age the same way humans do, my mother, grandmother, and I could be mistaken for sisters. If we were ever in the same room at the same time, anyway.

"Save the trash talk for the other team, Aunt Mag, and try not to break a hip."

You can't really say you've been flipped off until an old lady gives you the bird.

The backyard which, thanks to the power of a faerie engorgement charm had quadrupled in size, now featured an entire football stadium, complete with the smell of hamburgers, fries, and freshly-mown grass.

One faerie stood near each corner of the field, tossing a football back and forth across a hundred yards with casual flicks of the wrist any NFL quarterback would envy. Terra, my official godmother, hopped daintily to pluck the ball from the air about twenty feet above her head of flowing, earth-toned locks. Flipping in the air and landing in a somehow graceful crouched position, her granite eyes shined mischievously from above high, petal-pink cheekbones.

Vaeta pulled a coin out of thin air, flipped it up to spin effortlessly, and pointed a finger at Salem, "Heads or tails?"

"Tails!" He called out the obvious choice for a feline as she caught the quarter in her palm and flipped it over onto the back of her other hand.

"You win, do you want the ball now or after halftime?"

Salem chose the safer option and tossed the football to Mag, who pulled our team into a huddle and laid out our first play. "Lexi, you're QB; Vaeta and Terra, I need you on guard against your sisters. Don't let Lexi get sacked."

We took our positions and, as instructed, I pretended to hand the ball to Salem, who streaked quicker than a wink toward the defensive line. With all eyes on the flurry of black fur, I surreptitiously passed to Mag, who hopped down the right side of the field to get the first down plus a gain of another five yards. This from a woman who couldn't scoop her own ice cream at night because of her advanced age. We were going to have a talk about her manipulative ways.

Salem, extricating himself from a pile of faeries began to whine about how this was supposed to be touch football and not tackle but stopped himself when Pyewacket began fussing over him for taking the hit. Salem's chest puffed out a bit, and I swear I saw him flex his biceps at least three times.

"All right, all right, you can fawn over each other later, once we've won." Terra brought him back to earth.

Two short passes and a couple of runs later, we were on 4th and goal and had run out of diversionary tactics. "All I've done so far is protect Lexi. Let me take a stab at running." Terra insisted.

We all lined up again, and let me tell you, facing a fire and a water faerie in any capacity—the tackle taken out of the equation notwithstanding—is intimidating. Vaeta put up a wall of wind that blew Soleil's fire storm in the opposite direction while Terra slid into the end zone as if she were on ice skates, the earth at her feet rumbling into a blockade of stone that deterred any attempt to reach for her flag.

Faeries cheat. They see it as "making their own rules," but let's call a spade a spade. Once the cheating ice was broken, we were in the middle of a free-for-all.

"Touchdown!" Terra shouted, doing a little dance that would have looked dorky on anyone but a beautiful if slightly disheveled faerie.

"All right, now you've asked for it." Gran hiked the waistband of her sweatpants up a notch, snapped the ball and threw a bullet straight to Evian, who erected a water barrier in front of Jinx to send him running for cover in the other direction. Even in human form, the familiars hated water.

"Dirty move," I yelled, bending over and motioning to Vaeta, who hopped, skipped, and jumped onto my back to dive in front of Evian, a funnel cloud of wind turning the water barrier to mist.

"First and ten on the fifteen-yard line!" Gran shouted in triumph. They were about to tie it up, and even though the rest of us were playing in good fun, I could tell the faeries' competitive nature was starting to get the better of them.

Sure enough, Soleil got possession of the ball and pushed her way to the end zone in a rolling sphere of fire none dared counter. She did her own little dance and high-fived the rest of her team before Gran kicked the ball back down the field and we began our next drive.

Soleil and Evian held Vaeta and Terra at the line of scrimmage, earth and wind pressing fire and water away from where I stood in the pocket, searching for a receiver. Gran had Mag pinned to the ground, all pretense of a peaceful tackle-free game having gone out the window.

Pye and Salem were doing everything in their power to keep the more spry Jinx from sacking me, and I realized I was going to have to carry the ball myself if we had any chance of scoring. With a deep breath, I took off at a sprint, bounding over Mag's prone figure as Gran raised her hand and grabbed hold of one of my shoelaces which had come untied at the most inopportune moment.

Fortunately, Vaeta's final attempt to assist me came in the form of one more gust of wind, which I rode into a somersault and landed on my feet ready to take off down the field.

The wall of sound slammed into me as if I'd pelted full tilt into an actual wall. My hair blew straight back, and then, so did I. Three or four running steps backward, and I landed in a dazed heap with the pigskin lying on my chest.

"What is that horrible noise?" I couldn't imagine who might be blowing a foghorn on a day this clear, or this far from port. Or this freaking loud.

"Sorry. I've been waiting for this call, so I cast a little amplifying spell on my ringtone." Gran's focus slid toward Mag, and I read excitement along with an odd reluctance in her expression before I scrambled back to my feet. Aunt Mag avoided my attempt to get her attention, so I shot Terra a questioning look. If anyone knew what was going on, it would be the undisputed queen of household gossip. All I got back was a half shrug that amped my curiosity up another level.

Ten minutes passed while we waited for my

grandmother to return, and when she did, her face gave away nothing. The game resumed, and only because I continued to watch while seemingly remaining uninterested, did I see Aunt Mag and her sister exchange a glance that spoke volumes. Whatever the call had been about, it put a smile on both their faces and a glint in their eyes.

Chapter 8

My promise not to return to Deli Delight rendered null and void by the jerk I'd made it to—yes, I was getting to the anger phase in my breakup grieving process—I had just bitten into the crunchiest pickle in existence when the door to FootSwept opened without the usual polite knock.

"What are you doing here?" I left a film of salty brine on the button mounted under the lip of my desktop when I tapped out the SOS. How it worked, I had no clue since there were no wires or other connections to the button, but it never failed to bring Flix when I needed him. Unless we were fighting and even then, I doubted he would ignore the distress code.

"Can't I pay my dear sister a visit without reliving the Inquisition?" Jett looked like the cat who swallowed the canary, and I wondered whether he was daft enough to think I'd forgotten his conversation with Serena and the way he'd relished the idea of taking me down a notch.

"Get out of my office." I spat and stood to look my brother square in the eye. "Now." Lightning flickers arced between fingers itching to work up a good hex to throw at him. Self-defense shouldn't come with magical consequences, right?

Jett lifted an eyebrow at me. "Or what? What exactly will the great Lexi Balefire do to me if I don't vacate the premises?" He leaned against the door and crossed his arms; fixed me with a defiant stare that made my blood boil. "Don't you want to know why I stopped by?"

"I'm assuming you're here to do one of the only two things you ever do: make idle threats or whine about how our father loved my mother more than he loved yours." Jett's face paled, and his self-righteous smirk disappeared. "Get over yourself and grow up," I added for good measure.

A sneer twisted his face. "Your mother was a…"

The air pressure changed when Flix walked through the connecting door leading to his salon and made his way across the room. I felt the tremble of banked power running through the hand that dropped to soothe my shoulder and assure me he had my back. Literally, at the moment.

"Trixie sends her regards." Referring to my childhood obsession with Trixie Belden, a fictional sleuth featured in a set of books I'd unearthed from a box in my mother's closet when I was young, Flix let me know he'd not been ignoring my call. He'd been listening behind the door before making his entrance.

"Striker." His voice boomed with a resonance only the Fae can achieve, and then only when they really want to make a point. "Back to pick a new vacation spot? I have a couple in mind that I think would suit your needs. You prefer sun or snow?" Flix used a sardonic expression to get his point across. One that said he would brook no further threat from Jett and the next time he sent my brother to the Faelands, it would indeed be a one-way trip. "Or did you spend the last few weeks coming up with a good "your mama" slam to throw at Lexi?"

I watched, for the first time ever in my presence, Jett gather his faculties and resist hurling an insult back at Flix. Perhaps his time in Faerie had taught him a lesson or two in self-control.

"Actually, I came to deliver a message from her."

My eyes flicked from Jett's face to Flix's and back again, "A message from who now?"

"Your mother. Sylvana." Jett enunciated every syllable, relishing the opportunity to catch me off guard.

"You expect us to believe you've been in contact with Lexi's mother? After the way she treated Kin, what makes you think Lexi wants to hear from her? Or that we'd believe Sylvana would trust someone like you with sensitive information." Flix glanced in my direction again, and we had one of our unspoken conversations. He'd never say it out loud, but the thought of my disloyal mother cavorting with the likes of Jett wasn't entirely out of the question.

Jett got down on one knee, pulled a pocket knife out of his jeans, and pressed the tip to the center of his palm until a few drops of blood trickled over the blade. "Give me your hand."

"Why on earth would I do that?" Something was going on here that I had no idea about, but Flix did.

"It's all right, Lexi. Do as he says." Flix's posture had changed, and he'd gone from the offensive to a bored sort of resignation laced with irritation. "It's a blood oath. He's not going to cut you."

Jett looked almost as disgusted as I felt when I placed my fingers in his blood-stained hand, but the sensation didn't last long because as soon as our palms touched a rumble of magic shook the room and I was mesmerized by the sound of my mother's voice booming through the space.

"Please Lexi, listen to me just this once—you already have everything you need to defeat the Darkest Heart. The answer lies within." That was it; no apology, no further instructions or helpful suggestions. Of course, my mother would send some cryptic message that made no sense to me whatsoever.

"Told you so. And now I've upheld my end of the

bargain, repaid my debt, and am free of you and your train wreck of a family."

Instinct took me over. Checked my brain out like a library book and before I realized what I'd done, I was holding the Bow of Destiny in my hand. Not the ethereal, light-filled Goddess, but me, Lexi. The flesh and bone witch cupping the rock-solid shaft of an arrow nestled into the taut string—aimed and ready to fire.

"Don't push your luck, because I'd just as soon shoot you as look at you, and I'd be perfectly fine if instead of finding your true love you found out the same thing our father did when it happened to him."

I never meant to tell Jett about the real events on the day our father walked off and left his prized possession behind. For one, I didn't want to turn Gran into a target—though it would be worth it to see Jett try for her. Green and warty might look good on him. Secondly, I liked having something in my back pocket after he'd found such glee in knowing things about me that I didn't even know myself.

But the truth was, Gran had been responsible for Cupid's unexpected, wordless departure from this realm. She'd given my father a taste of his own medicine during the debacle that had banished my mother and ended with Gran being stoned for two and a half decades. When I thought about it in those terms, I understood why my grandmother had suffered the consequences with dignity—she felt like she deserved them, even though her intentions had been noble.

Naked greed washed over Jett's face at the sight of the living gold glinting in my hands, but for once, he had sense enough to rein himself in. What would happen if I loosed an arrow at him was anyone's guess, and it seemed he was as loathe to find out as I should have been. At the moment, I was playing eenie-meenie-miney-mo in my head. Seemed like as good a way to decide as any.

Practically spitting fire, Jett stepped forward, "That's mine, you have no right to…"

"One more step, Jett. I'm not kidding." I said through gritted teeth.

"…my father's possessions." He stopped. His hands fell to his sides.

"Sorry, brother, I guess you'll just have to deal,"

"Forget it. I didn't come here to fight. You just seem to bring out the worst in me."

"Right back at you, big brother. Now get out."

If there was a hint of admiration in the look he threw over his shoulder on his way out the door, it had to be a trick of the light.

Going home and acting normal after the horrible day I'd just experienced threatened to sap up every ounce of energy I had to spare. Avoiding the unholy combination of godmothers, grandmother, and intuitive aunt until I felt more settled seemed like a good idea.

Salem would pounce and demand I work on honing my magic the second I stepped into the workshop, and I no longer had a second home with Kin, so unless I wanted to dump out this new bag of wacky for family inspection, I needed some time to sort through it before going home. The emotional shrapnel would just have to work its way into my soul until I could find a pair of tweezers big enough to remove it without losing any more of myself.

So, I turned to the one other person who shared my dislike of Jett.

"Men suck." Serena waved her virgin daiquiri in my face. After a second unsuccessful round of *where's the talisman*, we'd taken our bonding ritual to the nearest bar.

"Beyond the telling of it. You know, I could fix you up with someone better than my jerk of a brother." A haze of alcohol momentarily glossed over the reason we were there in the first place. To celebrate how much we thought men suck.

"Dating isn't on my current to-do list." The dry comment fell on drunk ears. "*I'm pregnant with a godling child* makes lousy fodder for first date conversations. I've got enough on my plate as it is."

"Besides, men suck." I toasted the sentiment again. "You could always call Diana Diamond if you don't think I'm up for the challenge. The way things are going, I'm starting to think my clients would be better off letting the Queen of Hearts take over."

Serena snorted, "Stop whining. It's not attractive, even on you. And there's something off about that Diamond woman. Really off. She gives me the creepy vibe, you know what I mean?"

Every witch comes into the world with an affinity for at least one area of the craft. Divination, spell casting, heightened intuition, the ability to fashion tools of unfathomable strength. Having been part of a decade-long feud with Serena, I had no idea whether hers was an actual affinity for seeing the heart of a person or if her upbringing had fostered a reluctance to trust people. Either way, she was spot on about Diana Diamond.

Nabbing the cherry on a plastic skewer from her drink, Serena said, "When I'm ready, you'll be my first phone call. What I really don't want is to end up in a relationship like my parents. My mother thinks my father is worthless because he has no power, begging the question of why she ever married him in the first place. I swear, she's scowling in their wedding photos."

Because families fascinate me, I had to ask. "Was it always like that?"

"I've never heard her speak a good word about him, and I've always had the impression she has some kind of hold over him considering he appears to hate her with as much passion as she hates him. What kind of life is that?"

"They're definitely not soul mates, I could tell that from the first time I visited your house. And I was only six years old."

"It wouldn't take a magical matchmaker to figure that out." Serena spit with disgust. "Great role models. I think I always knew Jett didn't actually care about me. But at least there weren't going to be any surprises when his true colors finally came out. Pretty pathetic, huh? And now I'm stuck raising his kid all by myself."

I placed a hand on top of Serena's, something I never in a million years thought I'd do in a display of comfort. "You're not alone, and you're not pathetic. You've responded to what life has thrown at you, but that doesn't mean you're doomed to make the same mistakes."

"Doesn't it, though? Seems to work out that way for most people. Or are you the exception to that rule?"

I thought about Serena's question for a long minute. "I chose an alternative path to my mother's and went with the gettable guy. The guy who was *supposed* to be mine. I just assumed soul mate equaled euphoric, trouble-free relationship and didn't realize *happily ever after* is baloney."

"We're dealing with broken hearts here, I think we're past euphemisms for bullshit. Live a little, Lexi."

"In that case, I wish Kin Clark was the biggest asshole in four counties. Maybe then this wouldn't hurt so bad." I took the last swig of my daiquiri and suppressed a scrunched-up expression when I realized all the rum had settled to the bottom of the glass. "One more, bartender."

I swear I didn't mean to use a persuasion charm on the short, prematurely balding man to speed up the process, but my inhibitions were slightly lower than usual, and I figured karma owed me a favor.

"It still would. It always does. Sometimes it hurts more to be rejected by someone who wasn't even worth your time. And besides, the fact that Kin was willing to give you up means he definitely wasn't worth it. Obviously didn't know what he had."

Did Serena just compliment me? My brain had trouble taking it all in. Might have been the daiquiris though.

"You should take your own advice, Snodgrass." I leaned in and bumped her shoulder with my own, bestowing upon her the gentle smile of the truly hammered. "You're not nearly as repulsive as I always thought you were."

"Gee, thanks, Balefire."

"Can I tell you something?" I was about to confide in Serena Snodgrass, who I'd called every curse word in the book and nearly killed with dark magic once upon a time. Another one of life's little surprises. Serena nodded and motioned for me to continue.

"I've never had a real boyfriend before Kin. Not

someone whose soul mate I couldn't sniff out within ten seconds of meeting him. That's pathetic."

"To two pathetic women and their pathetic love lives." Serena raised her virgin drink, and we clinked before taking a sip.

"Lexi Balefire is not pathetic." A voice hissed into my ear, causing me to whirl around and nearly spill my drink.

"Mona!" I exclaimed, realizing how happy I was to see her after having avoided her calls and texts for weeks. "And you don't know the half of it. Have a seat. This is Serena."

"Pleased to meet you," Mona leaned forward to make eye contact.

"Nice to meet you, too." Serena's face closed off, and I wasn't so wasted that I didn't notice and wonder why. "Next round is on me."

Mona softened. "Thanks. Lexi, why haven't you been answering my text messages and voicemails?" Mona demanded. "I know that whatever is going on with Kin is tough, but I'm still your friend, and I miss you."

"I miss you too, Mona, I've just been wallowing in self-pity while the love of my life takes up with the bleached blond bimbo from hell. Does Mark know anything about this?"

I felt no shame about asking; that's what girlfriends are for.

"Mark is as baffled as I am. She's horrid, and he's

acting like a zombie. It's like he's under a spell or something." I nearly spit my drink across the table and exchanged a wide-eyed look with Serena. "I know he still loves you though, Lexi, I just don't know what he's thinking right now."

"Well, you could have fooled me. Maybe Kin just doesn't want to deal with me and my issues anymore."

Mona looked at me like I was crazy, "What issues? You're the most put-together person I know."

How she could say that after being present for more than one meltdown when the complications of my life got out of hand, I'll never know.

"And besides," Mona continued, "we all have our problems and our baggage. But love is enough to conquer all. Sometimes it just takes a bit of hard work."

It should have been *me*, daughter of the God of Love, spewing lines like that, but my confidence had begun to waver in the wake of personal tragedy. They say you shouldn't take your personal life to work with you, or vice-versa. It's a little more complicated than that in my case.

Serena rolled her eyes, "Pfft. I'll trade problems with either one of you any day of the week. What's going to be hard work is raising this baby by myself. Some people just don't want to put in the effort. Doesn't sound like Kin wants to put in the effort any more than my ex-boyfriend does. Lexi's better off."

It felt like I had the devil on one shoulder—okay

make that barstool—and the angel on the other, and at the moment, I couldn't help agreeing with my more bitter friend. It's easy to spout off platitudes when you're in a loving relationship with a man who worships the ground you walk on. I was eternally happy for Mona, but this is why single girls stick together. It's much harder to cultivate cynicism when hanging around with someone who always thinks the glass is half full.

As if things couldn't get worse, my half-brother chose that moment to walk into the bar. I was beginning to wonder if Jett had me bugged. Or maybe Serena.

"Incoming," I nudged Serena and tilted my head in Jett's direction. Sheer terror crossed her face as she tried, unsuccessfully, to melt into the floor.

"Oh, no." Understatement of the year.

"Well look what we have here. You're still slumming it, I see, Reen." Jett opened with an insult and I worried my shaky hold on self-control might not be able to handle two confrontations with my brother on the same day. The only saving grace was the fact that we were in a public place, and Jett knew better than to reveal our witchiness to normal humans, regardless of his contempt for anyone non-magic-bearing. "Let me know when you're ready to play with the big boys again."

I snorted. "Think much of yourself, sparky?"

A protective hand dropped instinctively toward Serena's belly, and if it weren't for that gesture, my idiotic brother might not have picked up on the fact that the extra weight she was carrying had nothing whatsoever to do with drowning her sorrows in too many pints of ice cream.

"Wait. Are you? Is that—?" Jett sputtered, and even though this wasn't a laughing matter, the copious amount of alcohol I'd consumed felt differently. His flabbergasted expression took on an aspect of high comedy and I felt a case of the giggles threatening.

"Why didn't you tell me?" He grabbed Serena by the arm, not hard enough to hurt, just to get her attention. He'd have done better to poke a sleeping bear. Less dangerous than a pregnant witch.

Serena launched off the barstool like it was made out of springs and poked Jett in the chest so hard he took two steps backward. Magical energy prickled over my skin and suddenly, I wasn't quite as drunk anymore and the case of the giggles was gone.

"Exactly when was I supposed to tell you? When you used me for your own nefarious purposes? Or maybe when you got sent to…" Serena realized she was in public and caught the word Faelands before it fell off her tongue. "…sent away."

She poked him again, and her shrill tone caught some attention. "Or maybe when you came back weeks ago and didn't bother to tell me. Now you're here looking at me like I'm the one hiding things from you? Don't come around again. I have nothing more to say to you." With a final poke, Serena turned back to the bar.

"I've got to get out of here. Now." She grabbed her purse, and when she turned back around, Jett was gone. "Or maybe not." Then Serena burst into tears. "I thought he'd put up more of a fight than that," she wailed, her voice going up into a squeak at the end.

"Men suck." It was the best advice I had at the time.

Walking Serena home sobered me up a little more, though clearly not enough. I helped her form a complex series of wards around the house after we made sure the place was empty. That's a lie—I contributed next to nothing to the process before wobbling off toward home.

Chapter 9

It's not breaking and entering if you have a key, right?

Too many strawberry daiquiris had loaned me a dose of liquid courage, and when I passed by Kin's street on the way home from Serena's, I impulsively decided to gather the rest of my belongings and hammer the final nail into the coffin of our relationship.

I slid through Kin's front door under the cover of a darkness spell that killed my ability to declare the act of trespassing a mere technicality. Witchlight blooming in my palm, I made my way to the bedroom to see if her things had taken the place of mine. Did she have a drawer already? Was her toothbrush in the cup on the edge of the sink? Would it hurt more or less to see it there?

Stupid idea, I knew, and I marched into the bedroom anyway.

One suitcase belched its contents over the rumpled bed, two more cluttered the doorway to the walk-in closet. Both ones I recognized from the week in a hotel I'd managed to spend on Kin's tour before he met Miss Belly Ring.

Bubble-headed bimbo. True love's kiss should mean something.

The emotional distance between devastated and totally pissed off is small enough to swing back and forth between the two in a matter of seconds. My heart bounced between my stomach and my throat like a demented rubber ball, and I couldn't get a handle on whether to cry or scream. Or both.

By any commonly-accepted description, a relationship goes through an orderly set of stages that starts with a meeting and spends months, maybe years leading to a bonded relationship. Kin and I rocketed right past all the preliminary stuff when I ended up releasing him from a curse by sharing a kiss that turned out to be magical and of the true love variety. I would never tell him this, but going from relative strangers to a fated match took some of the fun out of our courtship. Then again, maybe he felt the same, and that's what had led to this new relationship.

Maybe it wasn't at all odd that he'd fallen out of love with me just as quickly as he'd fallen in.

No. That's insane. You don't tell someone you love them one day and then dump them the next.

And what made me think I was so special that I couldn't get dumped anyway? The pendulum of wacky in my head swung back to the other side, and my slightly inebriated state only increased its speed.

I pulled one of Kin's shirts out of the suitcase and buried my face in it, breathed in his unique scent. A hint of wood smoke over a sharp, almost salty tang, and lime. He'd been using the aftershave I made for him out of essential oils and a touch of magic to keep his face from chafing.

The scent twisted my guts into knots and my tears darkened the cotton to midnight blue. How could it be over? Without warning. Without anything. Just over.

Covering my face with both hands, I pressed my palms to over my eyes and wondered how I could feel so empty and yet so full of pain. Going to Driven was a mistake, and I needed to get out of there fast.

When I tossed the tee back into the case, a flash of white caught my eye and drew my hand to pull back the pile of items far enough to reveal a playing card tucked into the side of the suitcase. Not just any card, either. The queen of hearts, and it had an all-too-familiar logo emblazoned across the front.

Hot tears turned cold along with my blood. Diana Diamond. What on earth was this doing here?

Well, duh, Lexi, I told myself. Kin must have gone to her for help with finding someone else.

The sound of my world crashing down around me

was surprisingly quiet. A soft noise like a sob riding a slow breeze. A few seconds stretched into a minute, and then I reached for the card intending to tear it into confetti.

My fingertips closed around the queen of hearts, mist rose up to surround me in cloudy gray tinged with pink as witch met Goddess to pull me into a vision unlike any I'd ever experienced before—and I've Seen a few things since Awakening as a witch, so that's saying something.

This time, I was a passenger in someone else's memory rather than a silent, unseen, shimmering observer. My arms were sheathed in black velvet narrowed to a point at the knuckles of my middle fingers, and I could actually feel the form-fitting leather pants wrinkle against the backs of my knees as I crouched behind a row of shrubs.

A complicated up-do piled too tightly on top of my head held the skin near the corners of my eyes so taught I couldn't have smiled if I tried. For the life of me, I couldn't fathom who would need to sport a black outfit complete with floor-length cape in the middle of what felt like summer.

Before I had a chance to ponder the thought any further, the body I was hitchhiking inside turned her head to focus on a couple walking toward one another, and when I saw the garden gnomes, I realized our stiletto boots were grinding my next door neighbor, Mrs.

Chatterly's, petunias into mulch.

My heart leaped into my throat while no-name with the trashy outfit clenched her fists and held her breath as the couple I now recognized as myself and Kin locked eyes for the very first time.

It's incredibly unnerving—and in this case, overwhelmingly painful—to watch yourself doing something you've already experienced, and even more so when the memory is a cherished, frequently-visited one.

Glowing, pink heart symbols blossomed in the air above our heads, and even though I already knew we had been destined for one another, it was a relief to have confirmation of the fact. If I'd been looking at two strangers, I'd have pulled out the Bow of Destiny and pierced both their hearts right then and there.

The sad part was, Kin and I wouldn't be in this mess if, during the moment I was reliving from six months prior, the bow had been in my father's hands rather than encased in a magical repository waiting for me to find and wield it.

Had we both been pierced by one of Cupid's—now my—arrows before experiencing true love's kiss, our bond would have been unbreakable. Unfortunately, I can't train the bow's sight on *myself*, and wouldn't have seen the symbols if I'd had it in my possession at the time, anyway.

My right hand reached beneath the cloak and

reappeared holding a deck of cards. With all the dexterity of a magician, the hand flipped through the stack to choose a particular card. She held it aloft, index finger pressing into one corner the way you clutch a flat rock you're about to fling across the surface of a calm lake.

My eyes narrowed and homed in on the me from the past, and a feeling of loathing toward myself oozed from my host's very core. Loathing that quickly gave way to disciplined patience and a dark void as I watched myself hurry into the house leaving Kin staring after me with stars in his eyes. Despite the agony of watching the tender moment play out, I was deeply grateful for whatever magic had brought me to this place. Whether Kin loved me anymore or not, his feelings at that moment had been written all over his face.

The scene faded to black, and when I was able to see again, I was standing in the crowd at a familiar nightclub; Driven, the place where Kin had been discovered by the rock band he'd left town to join. It was also the place where my ex had played the night Jett's love spell almost got him killed. My host's gaze traveled from Kin, who was just about to get attacked by a mob of lusty women, to where I stood by the edge of the stage.

I remembered that exact moment, trying to decide whether Kin deserved my help or not; whether he had been the one to bespell his guitar so that any woman listening to him play became instantly infatuated with the man strumming the strings. But now, trapped inside a body that wasn't mine, experiencing someone else's emotions, all I felt was my companion's wrath as she watched me come to my senses and realize I loved Kin and would do anything to keep him safe.

I felt her anger and frustration as vividly as if it were my own. When past Lexi hauled past Kin out the back door of the club and toward our destiny, she couldn't swallow the fury, and I felt it bubble into the back of her throat like bile.

The vision swirled again; we stood outside my home the very next night, and when a beam of white light burst through the Balefire house roof, I knew I'd just witnessed the effect of my true love's kiss with Kin.

A wave of vile loathing swept through the mind and body in which I rode, washing everything in its path with the kind of darkness that echoed with cries of the forlorn. The depth of pure hatred could have swallowed my house and still had room for more.

Scene after scene flickered by, each one more bittersweet than the last. Whoever I was traveling with hated me with a fiery passion, and wanted me to feel as much pain as possible. To say I felt violated is an understatement. Someone had been following Kin and me; watching us and planning to launch an attack. By the time the last portion began, I had already figured out what the ending would be.

Kin, alone on tour, walking into a convenience store, fingers flying over his screen with the last text he sent me before radio silence; the one I received after picking up sandwiches at Deli Delight.

Phone tag. You're it…

He paid for his purchases and stepped through the door with a smile on his face. My glance involuntarily flicked to a woman juggling two shopping bags and attempting to wrestle her keys from inside a large leather purse sliding off one shoulder. Her blond hair hung in a waterfall of curls, sheathing her face from my view, but the undulating black heart above her head didn't escape my attention. A greasy smear, the exact opposite of glowing pink.

My host's hand moved against my will, whipping out a playing card from beneath the billowing robe to fling it at Kin's heart like a ninja's kunai.

When it hit, he stopped dead in his tracks, stiffened for the length of a breath and I felt my lips curl up into a delicious smile as I watched him walk toward the blond woman and relieve her of her bags. A few moments into their hushed conversation, Kin's phone rang and he bent his head forward enough for me to get a clear view of the face under all that blond hair. It was Rachel, the bimbo from Walgreens, and Kin had just sent my return call to voicemail.

A wicked, depraved laugh echoed in my head, and when she turned to take her leave, and I caught my host's reflection in the convenience store window, I finally got to see who was responsible for Kin's current condition. It came as no surprise when all I could do was mimic the smile on Diana Diamond's smug face.

When the vision ended, I took a good long look at it before I tucked the card into my pocket where its cold energy seeped into my thigh. The queen was more than Diana's calling card, it was her weapon. A weapon that was used *on* Kin rather than *by* him.

I know it was a flimsy hope to cling to, but it was the only one I had. If Kin were a victim of Diana's will, then I would find a way to break her curse and set him free so he could come back to me.

As if my thoughts had conjured the man himself, I heard the front door open and the bright sounds of Rachel's laughter punctuated by his deeper tones. She might be an innocent in all this, but I had trouble feeling sorry for the man-stealer. Women are ruthless like that sometimes.

Dousing my witchlight, I tried to come up with a plan to escape unnoticed.

Invisibility spell? Hide under the bed until morning? What if there were dust bunnies under there? Nope. I've had an irrational fear of them ever since I was seven and Terra enchanted the ones in my room to get me to clean up. I still have nightmares about balls of fur with pointy teeth.

Still, there were worse things to worry about. I

could not be in this room when they came upstairs. My heart could not survive seeing them together here. On the bed with the duvet cover I'd picked out.

This was one of those times when I cursed the gaps in my education. Witches at my power level knew how to slip through space with ease, and I couldn't even blame Salem for not teaching me how, since I'd spent considerable effort in ducking out of lessons.

Anywhere but here. Anywhere but here. The mantra echoed to the beat of my racing heart while I listened for the sound of steps on the stairs. I had never wanted anything more than I wanted to be anywhere but here.

I closed my eyes to concentrate on slowing my breathing before I passed out from anxiety.

Anywhere but here.

Nothing signaled the change; not a single sensation of motion or displacement until the trill of a night bird pulled me to blinking awareness. In the midst of desperation, I'd found the key to shifting places and I recognized the spot where I'd landed. My grandmother's stoned body once graced this place, and I felt like I understood a little better how she'd felt during that time.

Heavy and unable to move forward. Weighted to the ground with despair.

Chapter 10

"She's alive." Salem's voice rocketed into my skull like a bag of hammers. Jackhammers that is. My hands flew to my head in an attempt to keep it attached to my body, though at this point, cutting it off entirely might be preferable. If only to stop the pain. The sudden motion screamed through my back and shoulders.

"What happened? Was it an accident? How bad is it?" Voice slurring, memories blurred. I wasn't sure I wanted answers to those questions.

"Unless you accidentally poured half the alcohol in the city down your throat, it was intentional."

Oh. A hangover. The mother of all hangovers, apparently.

I cracked open one grit-encrusted eye, just the tiniest slit and groaned.

"Where am I?" Not in my nice soft bed, that much was certain. Something sharp bit into my left hip, and I smelled dust. For the love of all that is good and holy, don't let me sneeze, I prayed to any deity that might be listening. Was there a patron saint of the stupidly inebriated? Death by hangover might prove a real possibility if I did.

"Well, you're under the sofa. Half under, actually." I heard the distinct sound of my cell phone camera going off. "It's going to be your new wallpaper."

"You're dead. If I survive this, I'm killing you."

"Can you get out on your own or do I need to help you? I have some of Terra's hangover juice out here. She says it won't get all of it, but it should bring you down from a ten on the zombie scale to a solid three."

"I've got her." Vaeta's voice carried great sympathy along with hints of amusement. Why do people find hangovers funny?

"Go away and let me die in peace."

A jet of warm air slid under me, tickling as it went and lifting my body ever so slightly off the hard floor. In seconds, I'd been deposited on the sofa instead of under it, and Salem was pouring Terra's hangover knockout cure down my throat. It burned a path to my gut and soothed like a warm blanket. I felt a little bit like Frankenstein's monster, all my pieces getting stitched back together.

"Thanks." I pinched the bridge of my nose, opened my eyes all the way, and sighed with relief when the lids didn't make scratching sounds in my head. If I had known the entire household was clustered in the doorway, I might have just rolled into the fetal position and stayed under the couch. Salem and Vaeta witnessing my humiliation was bad enough.

"I'll just be in the shower for an hour if anyone needs me." I could stay in there until I turned into a prune thanks to the combination of Evian's water and Soleil's fire magic. Faerie living. Gotta love it.

"You'll eat first," Terra put on her best mother hen impression.

"And you'll tell us what brought on this stunning display of self-abuse," Gran insisted. There would be no slinking upstairs to plumb the depths of my shame in private.

"My memory is a little hazy." A small fib, because Terra's sure-fire hangover cure-all contained a clarity charm and she darned well knew it.

"You'll eat, and you'll talk."

I would—and then I planned on paying Diana Diamond a visit. That part I would leave out of the breakfast confession, though.

Fed, clean, and fortified by the righteous indignation of my family, I blew through the closet at FootSwept looking for the perfect outfit to wear when confronting an enemy. Clothes are the modern-day version of armor, and I needed to feel empowered by the choices I made with mine. Scoff if you will, I really don't care.

Twenty minutes later—okay, maybe more like forty-five, but I swear I'm not the high-maintenance type under normal circumstances—I was dressed, coiffed, and ready for battle. At least, the type of restrained battle that would take place between two supernatural beings when surrounded by a room full of unsuspecting humans.

My hair hung in a high, straight ponytail, a lock of it wrapped around the base to conceal the elastic band, and my eyes glimmered from between lids lined with kohl to create a smoky effect. I was going for put together, chic, and formidable in a black lace Dolce & Gabanna fall collection pencil skirt, matching three-quarter sleeve blouse, and patent leather Louboutins. Three inch.

Queen of Hearts occupied the corner office on the third floor of the Millennium building, a newer glass and concrete behemoth that ruined the aesthetic of Port Harbor's old world charm. Diana Diamond had a secretary, for Hecate's sake. How much of my business had the woman poached to require a full-time staff? I blew right past the receptionist and bearded the lion in her den.

Diana saw me coming, the walls were made of glass, and looked at me with a disdain so palpable I wanted to slap her across the smarmy mask covering her true face. Whatever flavor of supernatural scuttled underneath her slick surface, she kept the evidence well hidden.

We locked eyes for a moment—long enough for me to taste and test her non-human vibe. Not witch. Not Fae. Something else lurked, something familiar, but I couldn't pin it down when all my urges were directing me toward conjuring up some wicked magic.

"Why if it isn't Lexi Balefire, right here in my own little office. Come to storm the castle, did you?" If I'd had any doubts before, they puffed into smoke. Diana wanted a confrontation. Needed it, if the predatory glint in her eye meant anything.

"Take the spell off my boyfriend."

"And why would I do that?" All pretense fell away. I knew what she was, and Diana knew that I knew. And that's a lot of knowing for one day. "When it's such fun to watch you squirm."

The words *don't you know who I am* wanted to fly out my mouth. I bit down on the phrase of entitlement and what actually popped out was, "Please."

Way to go, Lexi. Show her your badassedness…or not.

Diana looked at me with self-satisfied pity in her eyes, "If you don't have what it takes to keep your man, maybe you don't deserve him."

The shot at my ability to keep a man should have enraged me, and for a moment I felt a swell of dark magic in my breast. But, underneath all the pomp and circumstance, I was still a woman and Diana's words struck a chord, arrowed straight through to the deepest, darkest places of my heart that felt she might be right.

And she knew it.

"Bored now." Diana fluttered a hand to indicate I was nothing more than a nuisance and should leave. "Don't cross me, Balefire. You won't win."

"We'll see about that," I gritted out from between clenched teeth and turned to stalk out of the office.

"This isn't just about me, Flix. It's about the future of FootSwept. I'm only one person, regardless of all my titles, and I can't possibly run a successful business when I've got an endless supply of enemies plotting against me. Not to mention the fact that if I can't figure out how to counteract her cards, I'll lose the love of my life. Permanently. How am I supposed to play Cupid if I let my own soul mate get snatched right out from under me?"

I rambled on while Flix picked the black olives off my slice of pizza. My feet shuffled across the shag carpeting as I paced, building up enough static electricity to send a shock up my finger each time I forgot not to touch the metal frame of Flix's ultramodern coffee table.

"The whole reason we started FootSwept was to satisfy the pull you felt before you got your magic and if you'll remember correctly, to provide me with an outlet for my empathic abilities. We've both since grown and changed; you've Awakened and then been given access to a weapon that essentially makes our matchmaking business obsolete. Would it really be the end of the world if we closed up shop?"

Flix's face remained impassive; it was a trick I knew well. He'd ask a tough question and give me absolutely no indication of his own feelings on the subject, ensuring my answer was mine and mine alone. What he didn't seem to understand was the fact that he'd asked the question in the first place was often enough for me to discern his opinion.

If he wanted out, why didn't he just say so? Did he? Part of my mind wanted to linger on that thought, but the rest was centered on Kin.

"It's just not fair!" I wailed, choosing to avoid the discussion of business when I was more sober and less emotional. "I miss him." Stated simply, the truth cut through me like a knife.

"I know, Lexi. I know." Flix pulled me close to his chest and let me snot all over his shoulder for a solid half hour before my eyes finally ran dry.

"I'm sorry. I know how much it hurts you when I cry."

"Actually, I've been doing some exercises to help me learn how to sort of turn the volume down. Though you *have* ruined my new Gucci button-down, and that's a tragedy all by itself." He teased, coaxing me into a slightly better mood.

Chapter 11

Every witch has a special place she goes to work her craft. For some, like my Aunt Mag, it's a hut in the middle of nowhere built from stone and thatch and magic. For others, it's a brightly-lit, herb-scented kitchen with a pantry full of nothing you'd ever find in a supermarket aisle. And for the Balefire clan, it's a hidden room that lies on the other side of the fireplace where the flames we tend lick and sizzle and feed the magic of all witchkind.

I am the latest in a long line of witches named for the blazing heart of the sacred Beltane fire. I am also its Keeper, a job I nearly lost when I Awakened so late to my power, the fireplace had threatened to grow cold. Dodged a bullet on that one.

Only those with Balefire blood running through their veins are able to tame and reach into the fire, pull the iron lever without burning themselves to a crisp.

Today I had neither the time nor the patience to observe the phenomenon with my usual appreciation and simply yanked the handle without ceremony.

A click and a creak opened the door into my sanctum, and the room jerked abruptly as I crossed the threshold. Ever since Gran and Mag had come to stay, the interior had evolved into a configuration that served us equally and simultaneously. Still, a few items rearranged themselves to suit my taste, and before I could stride all the way across the pentagram-engraved casting circle, all the furniture had ceased rattling.

And then I nearly slapped myself on the forehead, spun around and marched back to where the Balefire flickered merrily in the hearth.

Cards were made from paper. Had the rock/paper/scissors game taught me nothing?

Destroy the card, break the spell. Seemed logical to me.

It was worth a shot and, after all, isn't there some saying about how the most simple solution is often the correct one? Whatever dark magic Diana Diamond had charmed into that card surely couldn't withstand a magical flame. I'd seen the Balefire turn balls of yarn into the ash equivalent of a dandelion fluff quicker than you can blink and it certainly felt like I was about due for an easy win.

I held the card in my hand and with no other thought in my head besides *destroy it*, leaned in toward the licking flames. The Balefire twirled just out of my reach, banked low and edged further away each time I moved closer. If I didn't know better, I'd interpret the shuddering motion it was making as a shiver, though a cold fire is oxymoronic even in magical terms.

"What do you think you're doing?" Salem must have slipped through the passage while I wasn't looking because I nearly jumped out of my skin when he spoke into my ear.

"Hecate's petticoats, Salem, are you trying to give me a heart attack?" I asked, lowering the card I still clutched between my fingers. All right, maybe I used a more colorful expletive than Hecate's petticoats, but swearing is unladylike, at least according to Gran. I try to reserve it for the proper occasions—or when I'm really drunk and mad at the world.

"If that's what it takes. I could sense dark magic the second you walked through the front door, and now because you're absolutely abysmal at keeping up with your studies, I've had to take a break from my afternoon nap to stop you from making a kindergarten-level mistake."

"Well excuuuuse me for breathing, Salem. What cataclysmic mishap have you saved me from now?" I exaggerated the eye roll because even though Salem loves to dish it out, he can't take being mocked without turning into a petulant child.

"You know what, go ahead and see what happens if

you're too smart for my help." Salem stared at me in silence, licked his lips once in a supremely catlike gesture and raised one eyebrow in challenge. If this had been a less critical pursuit, I might have tried it out of sheer orneriness and ended up wasting my hope of breaking the spell on Kin in a fit of pique.

"Fine. You are the best familiar ever. Blah blah blah. This is important, so get to the point." I used to wonder if all witch-familiar relationships were as tumultuous as mine and Salem's, but now that I've spent some time with Pyewacket and Jinx I realize that it's just our personalities. Maybe the fact that I didn't get my magic until nearly a decade after I was supposed to has something to do with it. Perhaps in another ten years, we'll get along like gangbusters, but I fear we'll behave even more like an old married couple than we already do.

"First of all, you have some explaining to do. What is that and where did you get it? And why aren't you asking for help from your elders? What's the point of having three witches in this house if you're just going to go rogue?"

"That's a first, second, third, and fourth of all, Salem." I sighed and explained how I'd come across the offending item. I might have glossed over the B&E, though Salem probably would have commended me for that part considering he'd done some illegal pussyfooting through Kin's house himself. "Now get to the point."

"You're about to force dark magic into the Balefire. Don't you remember what happened last time someone meddled with it? The coven's reaction alone should be enough to dissuade you from making the same mistake twice. I'm sure between us we can come up with some way to isolate the type of magic used and neutralize it without any fallout."

"Don't you dare get the rest of the family in on this. They're all still flip-flopping between smothering me with love and plotting Kin's demise. Besides; the godmothers are out setting up for some hoity-toity million-dollar sweet sixteen party, and Gran and Aunt Mag are off doing whatever it is that's had them sneaking out of here at every opportunity." Their traveling cloaks had been getting a workout since before Thanksgiving.

"If they find out about Diana Diamond's plans for the love apocalypse, they'll go into defense mode and honestly, I think they're out of their depth here. You too, for that matter. This is god business, and that means I've got to handle it myself. It's an order, Salem, and you know what that means."

He did know, better than anyone, but had failed to mention my authority over his actions in our witch/familiar orientation. If I give a command, Salem has to honor it, no questions asked. I'm not entirely certain what the repercussions for disobeying me are, but they must be severe, or he'd never agree.

"Fine. But you're doing this against my advisement."

"You've made your point. And actually, you've made me realize something. If Kin and I were destined for a shot by Cupid's arrow, then I've got the perfect counter to any magic used against us—the Bow of Destiny itself. Add a little Balefire to the mix and how can I go wrong?"

I couldn't just shoot Kin now; I'd learned my lesson about taking aim when the little heart symbol wasn't present above my target. The last thing I wanted to do was make the situation worse.

I walked across the casting circle once more and tacked Diana's card onto the cork board where we post spells in progress and then backed up a few feet. Power welled inside me, familiar and comforting, and called to my own inner Goddess.

If this worked, I'd smother Kin with kisses before the sun went down and do other things with him in the dark.

"Focus your intent, at least." Salem chided as I twirled one through the Balefire, then set my flaming arrow, and peered through the sight at its target.

Thoughts of Kin swirled through my consciousness: the way he would place his hand on the small of my back when we walked through a crowd; the warm, fuzzy caress of his laughter at one of my jokes;

the intensity of our first kiss, and how each subsequent embrace pierced my soul and cemented our bond.

If nothing else came from this experience, I suppose I owed Diana Diamond a vote of thanks for exposing my true feelings for Kin. You don't know what you have until it's gone—not just a convenient song lyric, or cliché, but a home truth I'd ignored for far too long.

I thought about Kin—and let the arrow fly.

A shower of sparks arced forward in slow motion, then abruptly changed course and pinged toward a bookshelf full of ancient, leather-bound first editions. Salem squeaked, and I managed to aim a protective barrier around the treasures just in time.

It didn't stop the arrow, though; the flaming tip bounced upward, ticked back and forth across the glass-domed ceiling above the casting circle, mercifully only making contact with the wrought iron encasement, and then fell straight down and embedded itself in the center of the pentagram.

"For the love of tiny pickles, Lexi, you almost shot me! Now, will you call in reinforcements?"

"Not yet."

Two hours later, I'd exhausted every spell-breaking method I could think of, and a few made up ones besides. The card lay in the bottom of a cauldron and mocked me. At least I thought it did, it was hard to see because of all the smoke.

"I'm done," I announced to Salem who had stopped arguing and was now sitting stiffly in the farthest corner of the room with his dirtiest I-told-you-so expression on.

"Shut up," I said before he said a word. "What happens in the Sanctum stays in the Sanctum."

"Fine," was all he said, but he flashed back to cat form and presented me with a good shot of his rear as he twitched his tail out the fireplace ahead of me.

Chapter 12

"Lexi, have you spoken to Serena recently? I've prepared a new batch of tonic for her, but she hasn't been by to pick it up. Would you mind running it over? Your Aunt Mag and I have some business to attend to."

"What kind of business?" I asked, taking care to keep my tone neutral even though suspicion had risen up inside my gut and made my stomach churn in nervous anticipation. Sneaking in and out the house at all hours, whispered conversations. I don't like secrets—especially the kind that send my fertile imagination into frenzied flights of fancy.

"Coven stuff. Nothing major." The rapid-fire reassurance missed its goal by a mile, leaving me with the decision of whether or not to call out my grandmother on the fib. Think what you will, I didn't have the stones to do it. "Everything okay?"

"Perfectly fine. Don't you worry your pretty head."

Why is it when someone tells you not to worry, that's the first thing you do? Human nature—witch nature, not all that different in the end. If I'd had less on my mind, I might have pushed the issue harder.

"And don't forget the tonic, okay?"

"Already on it. I'll drop by on my way to work." I hoped Serena was getting along all right. I'd nearly forgotten her with one thing and another. She must be freaking out now that Jett knew about the baby. Some kind of friend I turned out to be.

I tripped up Serena's front steps, shivered as the icy chill of her wards scanned over me. Juggling an insulated cauldron full of viscous liquid in my hands, I leaned on the bell before cracking the door open a couple of inches.

"Serena, it's Lexi. Can I come in?" I called out, listening for any indication she was home. If not, I'd leave the tonic in the refrigerator and be on my way.

Muffled noises emitted from the living room, and I hollered a little louder in case Serena's mother, Calypso, was home. We didn't exactly get along, and the last thing I wanted to do was spend a second alone with the woman.

"Hello, Sis." I gasped when Jett stepped out of the shadows, prepared to drop the cauldron and use my power against him if necessary. "It's nice of you to stop by. Serena will be happy to see you." Not a trace of his nasty nature showed in the smile on his face.

"Who are you and what have you done with my brother?" Body snatchers? Personality spell? If that was the case, good for you, Serena, never thought you had it in you.

This nice guy act? I didn't buy it for one second.

Apparently, Serena's spine had gone missing again. And just when I'd started thinking maybe she had a lick of common sense rattling around in that head of hers.

"Where is she?" I demanded, my voice rising to shrill tones that betrayed emotional involvement.

"Relax, Lexi. I'm right here, and I'm fine." Serena stepped into the foyer, both hands wrapped around her bulging belly, which had grown another inch since I'd seen her last. Was it only a couple of days ago? Was that normal?

She looked at me expectantly, sorry for the pun, and it took a few seconds before I could form words.

"What is he doing here?" Was all I managed. Serena knew, more than anyone, how treacherous my half-brother could be. I'd forgiven her for colluding with him to hurt me once we'd finally dragged our grievances out into the open. And, even if Diana Diamond was the one behind the current kerfuffle, I didn't trust him as far as I could throw a unicorn. She should know better than to trust him, too.

"We're having a conversation about a possible reconciliation." She stated matter-of-factly, fixing me with a stare indicating the subject wasn't up for debate.

"Jett wants to help me raise the baby. This little guy or girl deserves to have two loving parents."

"Yeah, Sis, you've got me all wrong. My priorities have changed." In a day? Doubtful.

I've lived with faeries my entire life, and parsing validity from carefully concealed untruth has become somewhat of a specialty of mine. The Fae can't lie outright, but Jett sure could. If he called me *Sis* one more time, I might punch him in the nards. Shared blood notwithstanding, we couldn't have been cut from more different cloth. I didn't believe he had Serena's or the baby's best interests at heart.

And yet, there was an urgency in his tone that spoke of real desire; a yearning I wouldn't have expected. A thread of truth, maybe, to his words.

Is it fair to assume someone can't change, knowing that I, myself, had been reincarnated several times over? Judging a person's entire being based on a few negative actions smacked of cynicism and hypocrisy, but something in my gut said Jett shouldn't—couldn't—be trusted.

"Serena," I ignored Jett completely and spoke directly to her as if he wasn't standing an inch from her side, "You can't possibly believe he cares about you. If he had, he would have come and found you when he escaped from the Faelands. Instead, he's been off doing..." I thought about it for a second, "...I don't know exactly. Do you really want your child being raised by someone who has only ever cared about himself?”

I could tell my words were lost on Serena; saw the way her eyes slid to Jett's face, the raw hope that lived there and let her believe she might not be alone in the seemingly insurmountable task of raising a baby on her own. A magical baby, no less.

Like the misogynistic jerk he truly was, Jett interjected before Serena could even open her mouth. “I'm not going to explain myself. Where I've been is none of your business.”

“Actually, it is my business, considering you showed up here with my mother's words on your lips. Wanna tell me how that came about?”

“Not that you'll believe me, but I spent some time searching my soul and trying to make up for things I've done in the past. You must have noticed I've been helping with matches, trying to take some of the burden off you. Geez, I'd think you'd be grateful. Maybe toss me a thank you or something.”

His voice had turned to a petulant whine. I half expected him to say something along the lines of “it's not fair!” and stomp his feet like a two-year-old.

“As if I believe anything that comes out of your lying mouth.”

Helping me with my matches?

“Lexi, I'm the only one who needs to let go of what he's done. Don't tell me you wouldn't do the same for

Kin if he were to waltz in here and tell you he had made a terrible mistake.”

“That’s different,” I sputtered, “Kin is my soul mate, and he’s under a spell.”

Serena gave me the sympathetic head shake that translates as, “Aw, honey, whatever you need to believe.” At that moment, I needed to believe I could get through the next ten minutes without committing a crime worthy of being stoned—the punishment exacted upon a witch who murders one of her own. Irrevocable and immediate.

“Forget about Kin. Since when has Jett done anything for anyone’s benefit but his own?” My eyes slid over to my half-brother, searching for even a morsel of remorse.

“You said you forgave me, Lexi. Why can’t you forgive Jett too? You didn’t see what he was going through; the pain your father caused when he walked away from his son. I know for a fact you’ve done things you’re not proud of, and I know you’ve tried to make up for them. Doesn’t he deserve the same chance?”

What was I supposed to say to that?

“Jett has explained everything to me,” Serena sighed, “He’s sorry for what he almost did to Kin at Shadow Hold, and he has information that might be useful to you if you’re willing to hear him out. It’s about your parents.”

“Funny he’s been in my face, what? Three times

now and this is the first I've heard about him being sorry. And about my parents, he's already told me everything he's going to—and if he hadn't made a blood vow, he would have kept the information to himself just out of spite."

Jett hated Sylvana even more than I distrusted her—and without the family ties to soften the blows of her selfish nature. He'd made the vow, so he must have had a good reason to need her help. Obviously, he'd managed to survive his forced vacation to the Faelands with few problems, considering he was still in one piece. Maybe the Unseelie race mistook his dark heart for one of their own.

As soon as that thought crossed my mind, something inside me screamed that I didn't see the bigger picture. Obviously, Jett cared about *something*, or he wouldn't have traded information with someone he loathed even more than me. From his skewed perspective, it had been my mother who took his father away and Jett wanted nothing more than to get his daddy's approval.

And back around to where I began; I couldn't get within a mile of Jett without drawing the same conclusions I always did. I saw a slimy snake with enough acting chops to dupe Serena, but not me. "He's not your soul mate, and you deserve better."

"That's for me to decide. I'm not saying I've forgiven him completely, but he is the father of my baby, and I owe it to all three of us to consider what he has to say. If you can't accept that, please leave." Serena's eyes pleaded for understanding, but it was more than I could give.

I shook my head sadly, set the cauldron of tonic on a low table near the door, and exited quietly. It would take more than words to convince Serena of Jett's true character. His intentions would make themselves known eventually. I just hoped it wouldn't be too late.

For now, Serena was on her own. I suddenly hoped Calypso would return and put a stop to this ridiculous charade, though I doubted her opinion would matter any more to her daughter than mine did.

Halfway home I spun in a semi-circle and headed back toward Serena's house. Almost to her front steps, I had third thoughts and turned once more in the opposite direction. Back and forth I debated, weighing the pros and cons of what I was considering doing. Eventually, curiosity got the better of me, and I decided it was time to flip the situation in my favor. I skulked between a pair of rhododendrons flanking Serena's front door and decided that since my stalking skills had been honed to perfection, I might as well use them to my advantage.

Fortunately, Jett only stayed inside for another half

hour, so I didn't have to wonder too long about what they might be doing in there. When he skipped down the front walk with a self-satisfied grin on his face, I trailed him to wherever it is scumbag demigods go at night.

It's a lot more difficult to follow someone under cover of darkness than in the light of day when other people are milling around, and Jett was too smart to be fooled by a glamour spell, so I had no choice but to keep a safe distance.

When he turned into a familiar alley between French Street and Hinge Avenue, I knew exactly where Jett was headed. The place where worlds meet is accessible from similar points in cities and towns around the world; there are probably entrances carved out of innocuous boulders on countless hillsides, for all I know. They all lead to a place where we beings entrusted with the knowledge that magic is just as real as the known laws of physics can let down the burdensome shields we're required to carry in the mortal world.

Of course, there are rules; you don't come to the Fringe and start peppering people with prying questions. It's kind of like Las Vegas. Harm none, do what ye will is more than a motto, and many have been ejected and banned either temporarily or permanently depending on the magnitude of the transgression. It was a double-edged sword; I could spy on Jett to my heart's content but knew better than to try and insert myself into his affairs.

I do find a certain amount of humor in the fact that the world between worlds is a giant carnival, though I have no desire to delve into the reason why it was created that way. Calliope music provided a backdrop to the hydraulic hiss of a four-story Ferris wheel's engine and the sing-song voices of carnies offering fantastic prizes in exchange for the opportunity to guess your age, weight, or shoe size or for you to guess theirs. I wouldn't have let the vast majority of them get close enough to smell my dirty socks, but if I closed my eyes, it sounded like any other fair or circus I'd ever been to.

The gods were smiling on me because I managed to avoid getting entangled in any verbal tugs of war with the persistent vaudevillians. Apparently, my brother wasn't as repulsive to everyone else as I found him to be. He stopped to drop a few dollar bills into a Dwarven bard's guitar case, waved a jovial hello to an old Orcish couple hawking charmed battle axes, and chatted with a foul-mouthed chickadee before ducking inside a black canvas tent with no sign or flag to broadcast its contents.

I circled around to the rear and hunkered down in a spot between the backs of three other tents where I wouldn't be seen, vehemently wished I had a pair of extendable ears and found a tiny hole to press my own regular one against.

The low-voiced conversation between Jett and a

creaky, feminine voice sounded a lot like the teacher from the Peanuts. Wah, blaw, wah, blah, wah. Out of the entire conversation, I caught only two words clearly. Talisman and blood. Enough to prove his intentions were as ignoble as I'd imagined.

Jett opened the flap and exited the tent with a whoosh, his legs carrying him across the midway at a faster pace than before. He made a beeline for yet another tent emblazoned with the name "Athena's Attic."

I counted my blessings, having visited the establishment during my last trip to the Fringe, because I happened to know there was a rear flap where I could enter unseen. A powerful Elven seer, Athena would undoubtedly sense my presence, but in accordance with the previously stated rule about interference, was unlikely to reveal my hiding place. I'd probably have to answer a half dozen questions about my intentions later, but for the time being, I was safe as houses.

"Good to see you, Athena." Jett's voice elevated to the pitch used by certain men when speaking to a woman, not exactly condescending, but infuriating nonetheless. "I need an Ardruvian tuning crystal and a packet each of dandelion root, nettles, and blue cohosh."

"Three days on the crystal. Herbs are over in the homeopathic section."

In a minute or two, the transaction complete, Jett

took his leave, and I trailed him back to Serena's.

Whatever Jett was up to, it didn't seem as though Serena was in any real danger—at least not at the moment, with the baby still months from full term—but I vowed to keep watch over her whether she wanted me to or not.

Chapter 13

"Get down!" I hissed to Flix, shoving myself behind a rack of Hawaiian shirts marked red for clearance.

"And boogie?" Flix fired back, not yet registering the urgency of the situation.

"Not funny. I thought you were an empath. Way to read the room." I jerked my head to the side to indicate he needed to move quickly or else he'd be spotted. But he moved to my side and made a disgusted face as his bare arm brushed low thread count cotton. What. A. Diva.

"Why would anyone buy their clothes at the same place they buy their dog food and toothpaste?"

I sighed, "Because most people's yearly clothing budget is closer to what you spend on toothpaste. Don't be a snob."

Big box stores are hated by lots of people. They're

crowded, and they love to hide those price scanner machines in dimly lit corners and then get annoyed when you ask for help. Unfortunately, they're also convenient, open late, and the one near me happened to stock the particular brand of blood orange sorbet that had been getting me through the last few painful days. I could just ask one of the godmothers to stock the freezer for me, but then I wouldn't get to enjoy the look on Flix's face as we cruised through the Men's section.

"What are we hiding from, anyway?" He spoke in an exaggerated whisper reeking of sarcasm and condescension.

"Kin and my acrylic-spandex-blend replacement. I can't deal right now." I shushed Flix and headed straight for the offending couple because well, that's what you do when you unexpectedly encounter your ex and his new girlfriend—stalk them—whether you want to know what's happening or not. It's a compulsion, and I'm sure I'm not the only former girlfriend who can attest to that.

Fear and pain trailed their gnarled fingertips around the edges of my heart, slowly creeping deeper as I stood my ground with difficulty.

"Hold still," Flix commanded, waving a hand to cast a glamour over both of us. Why didn't I think of that? "Now let's ditch this cart."

Under normal circumstances, I'd have cracked a rib laughing at Flix's choice of disguise. He must have been going for complete opposite because gone were the rippling biceps and chiseled facial features; instead, he sported a beer gut and a mullet. I took a quick look at my reflection in one of the chrome fixtures and smiled when I realized he'd made me a tall redhead with legs for days.

"People are going to think you're either ridiculously rich or my drunk uncle. Thanks for…" Flix, never one for warm and fuzzy feelings, waved away the words before I could finish expressing my gratitude for the attempt at humor.

"I'll be your sugar daddy for the next half hour as long as you swear never to tell Carl you saw me looking like this."

"Deal. Now let's go." We picked up the pace and headed toward where the love of my life had sauntered with his hand on another woman's backside. My heart thumped so hard I thought it might burst, and I resisted the urge to circle back to the sporting goods department for a shotgun. Not that I'd resort to violence. Maybe. I could wreak plenty of havoc all on my own, thank-you-very-much.

Rachel rested a garishly manicured hand on Kin's arm while they picked out a couple of porterhouse steaks at the meat counter, and it rankled on my last nerve. When he ran a finger down her spine, and she shivered with—dare I say it, desire—it felt like someone had punched me in the face. By the time they'd chosen a head of romaine and a loaf of crusty bread, I knew Kin was pulling out all the stops.

Steak and Caesar salad was his go-to seduction meal. He made it the first night I spent at his house, and the thought of him sharing it with someone else cut deep. Not that I'd seriously believed I was the first woman he'd wowed with his grilling skills, but I had definitely expected to be the last.

The hex slipped out of me in a cathartic rush. I would pay for it later, and I did not care. Not even a little. Those steaks were not going to get Kin into bed with his new sweetie. More likely she'd run screaming from the room when she got a look at their gooey, pus-filled centers.

Just for good measure, I gave the romaine a case of worms. Call me petty. Give me the t-shirt. I'll own it.

"Are you okay?" Flix asked, already knowing the answer.

I shook my head and continued following the pair to the wine section. When Kin reached for a bottle of my favorite Cabernet, I bristled. It was more than I could stand.

Flix grabbed me by the elbow and hauled me down the aisle, "I can't deal with all the angst, let's get out of here."

As I brushed past Kin, our skin touched for a fraction of a second. Images rose unbidden to fill my mind, but this was no Fate Weaver vision. Just memories from the past; our life together flashing by in the kind of movie-style montage they play when someone is seconds away from dying.

The day I met Kin on the sidewalk outside my house. Our first kiss; the way he'd cupped my face in his hands and pressed his full, perfect lips to mine. Kin chasing me through his kitchen, my hair tickling his back as he hoisted me over his shoulder and carried me to his bedroom.

All tender moments I feared I'd never again think of fondly. So what if I did break Diana Diamond's spell? Would that erase the image of Kin with Malibu Barbie? I'd probably never get her stripper perfume smell out of his sheets. We'd have to burn the house down. And even then, I wasn't sure.

"Kin?" Rachel's grating voice brought me back to the present, and when my eyes readjusted to the bright fluorescent lighting, I was standing face to face with Kin, and he was staring at me with soulful eyes, almost as if he could see past the glamour of the tall, gorgeous redhead to the devastated woman underneath.

Rachel's insistent arm patting pulled Kin's focus back to her, and he shook his head as if to dislodge a confusing image, allowing her to drag him away while she cast dark, narrow-eyed looks in my direction.

"Holy sh—Flix, are you okay?" I realized

mid-expletive that my best friend was rooted to the spot, his eyes unfocused. I touched his arm, and his head snapped to meet my gaze with a look of anguish.

"He's trapped in there."

"Excuse me?"

A quiver ran through Flix. "I could feel his pain, deep down, when you two touched. He remembers belonging to you and wants to again. It's hurting him and the past is slipping away. If it weren't for you two sharing true love's kiss, he'd be fine, but he's not. His soul is in such pain."

It felt like my body had turned to sand, and any second I would disintegrate, fall apart grain by grain until I was nothing but a pile on the floor to be tossed in the wind and swept away.

"You've got to figure this thing out quickly, or you're going to lose him forever."

We hightailed it out of the store, my sorbet forgotten, and rode back to my place in silence. Flix opened his mouth a few times as if he might speak, but took his cues from me.

"I just need some time alone. I'll call you later." I gave Flix a quick peck on the cheek while the engine of his sleek black Jaguar idled quietly in the driveway.

"Okay, Lexi. Whatever you need." He left with sorrow in his eyes. The experience had left him shaken. I knew the feeling.

"This isn't something you could have prevented, so don't beat yourself up. We'll fix it. We'll free Kin and take Diana Diamond down a couple of notches in the process. I just need to come up with a plan." I shooed him away and watched him drive slowly down the block.

Chapter 14

The encounter with Kin and Rachel necessitated a head-clearing walk, and if I hadn't been so caught up in my own thoughts, I might have heard the throaty purr of the Harley coming down the block before it rumbled to a stop beside me.

"Looks like the rumors are true. The once-great Lexi Balefire has been brought down by a man." Delta pulled off her helmet, killed the motor, and braced both feet on the ground, but stayed seated on the sleek dragon of a machine. It was so big, it seemed like my poor scooter would have almost fit in one of her saddlebags.

Delta's mocking tone did what nothing else had managed all day and dragged me from the depths of despair to the peak of pissed off in a record nanosecond.

"I thought you went back to Olympus in disgrace." Bounty hunting for the Gods was serious business, and Delta had experienced a little hiccup on her last job involving a Balefire witch. She'd been incredibly supportive of me, though, and I felt guilty sniping at her just because I was in a foul mood.

"There's hope for you, yet." Long and lean, dark and dangerous, Delta didn't just look bad to the bone, she lived up to the hype. I'd been on the business end of the sword she carried in a scabbard that rested down the length of her spine and stayed concealed beneath her clothes. Had she meant to kill me at the time, I doubt I would have seen much more than the glint of the metal before it pierced my hide. She was that good with her blade.

"Get on." Delta tossed me the helmet that appeared when she held out a hand, slid forward enough to leave plenty of room for me to climb on behind her, and I hesitated.

"You're not taking me to…"

"Don't be daft. Now climb on and let the wind and the open road blow your troubles away, or would you rather just keep trudging down the sidewalk?"

"Well, when you put it like that…" I grabbed the helmet and swung my leg over the seat. I'd barely found the foot pegs when Delta kicked the beast to life, and the powerful throb of the motor set a rhythm my heart tried to match.

Delta maintained a steady, even pace to the edge of the city limits, and then kicked the bike up to a roar as soon as the traffic dwindled enough for an open-throttled run. Even if it was only a temporary reprieve, my spirit soared with a sense of freedom. There was no Kin, no Rachel, no Diana Diamond out here—just the speed and the wind and the feeling of tearing up the miles.

For that time and in that space, the weight on my back lifted and I could breathe again. Given a choice, I would have kept going forever, but all too soon, Delta turned and rocketed back toward Port Harbor and home.

My knees felt wobbly from the constant vibration and the sudden lack of motion when I staggered back onto the pavement in front of my house.

"Got room for another warm body for the night?" Delta asked.

"Maybe. Probably. Things are in a state of flux around the house these days." Fracking chaos was closer to the truth, so I led the way onto the front porch. I settled with her on the swing, shoved all thoughts of my broken heart deep into my subconscious, and described the daily evolution and devolution of my home.

"The faeries keep building these elaborate additions for the elder witches," Gran would have a canary with a cotton tail if she heard me call her an elder witch, "who don't seem all that interested, so the next incarnation is meant to top the last. Something's up with that, and I don't have the energy to try and find out what's going on. It feels like a game of tug of war with me being the flag tied onto the middle of the rope."

Using my toe, I nudged the swing into soothing

motion.

"Never a dull moment, eh?"

"You ever planning to tell me why you're back?" I assumed her next mission had something to do with me. Everything does. Okay, that sounded really conceited. I only meant that my life has become a magnet for epic nuttiness, and I assumed Delta had been sent to sort me out. "Am I in trouble with—you know, I'm not sure how things work where you're from. Is there a committee? Or a hierarchy? Am I supposed to report to someone? Do you know where my dad is?"

Delta turned sideways, curled one leg under her, and said, "Whoa. Slow down. No one sent me, okay. You called me here."

The bald statement surprised me so much I stopped pushing the swing.

"I did? I don't remember calling you. How does that work exactly?"

She laid a hand on my arm.

"Look, give me a soft bed for a night or two, let those godmothers of yours feed me a generous helping of whatever it is I can smell through that door, and I'll tell you a story."

A guest would put the faeries on their best manners.

"As long as you know what you're getting into and go willingly, I'd enjoy the company." It surprised me how much. Without noticing, I'd become something of a social recluse since the day Kin came back to town with his new hussy.

It turned out neither of us had known what Delta was getting into. We figured it out, though, right about the time we glanced through the sliding door in the kitchen and saw a set of turrets complete with pastel pennants rippling in the breeze.

"Boy, when you people build onto a house, you really take it to the next level," she said.

"I told you. Didn't I tell you?"

Torn between the desire to clap my hand over my eyes and pretend I did not see the castle in my backyard or to go do something about it, I wasn't sure if I had the fortitude for either course of action. Under my adult facade, a remnant of Lexi, aged six, clapped and danced for joy. Demanded we go live out every girl's wildest fantasies and see if there was a room for us with a four-poster bed draped in pastel-colored chiffon.

"They read bedtime stories to kids about Cinderella and Snow White where you come from?" Giving in to my inner princess wannabe in front of a butt-kicking bounty hunter with no frame of reference? Nope. Not doing that. Probably.

I made a mental bargain with Hecate for the strength to resist temptation.

Delta shot me a crooked smile, her hawk-eyed gaze softened. "Not exactly, but I'm familiar with the concept." Dressed in motorcycle leathers over an outfit of basic black, she had more of a badass Barbie look than a Disney princess vibe. "I had a fling with one of the Grimm brothers back in the day."

Yanking my eyebrows back down from where they were about to tangle with my hairline, I tried to paste a worldly look on my face. I don't think I pulled it off.

"Oh. Hmm. Okay, then." Inappropriate questions about his basic grimness came to mind.

"He patterned one of the characters after me."

"Which one? Cinderella? Sleeping Beauty?"

"No, silly. The huntsman from Snow White." I guess I should have known.

"Still, I think we should go make sure the castle is…." Delta searched for an excuse, found them all flimsy, and said, "…I've got nothing. It's a castle. I want to go see it."

"Wild unicorns couldn't stop me."

A portcullis could, though.

"Anybody in there? Open up!" I called through the gate, my voice echoing off blocks of granite polished to a glittering shine. Pink granite. A pink castle. Couldn't you just swoon? "Come on, it's me, Lexi. Let me in."

"Might be easier if you just…" Reaching around me, Delta pushed the button marked Doorbell. How had I missed that?

Trumpets blared out a flourish of musical notes to announce our presence, and the portcullis slowly raised amid sounds of creaking wood and clanging metal. My heartbeat sped up a little with excitement. Was a backyard castle just slightly over the top? Well, yeah if Everest is the top you're trying to get over. Did I care? Nope. Not even a little. Maybe whichever faction—faeries or witches—was slated to live here would consider trading with me.

When the fireworks started, I assumed they were a welcoming measure. I should have known better. Before I had time to get a good look around, the ground shook hard enough to nearly knock me off my feet. Delta had her sword out and at the ready.

"Put that thing away," I knew what we were dealing with. "It won't do you any good if the faeries are in a snit."

"Snit?" The ground shook again. "Sounds like more than a snit to me."

"Unless a dragon bombs the ramparts, it's a snit. I've seen my share of them, and this seems like nothing more than the flash and boom type of fight. I should be able to diffuse it quickly. Follow me."

The grand castle tour would have to wait. If there was anything left to tour, that is. A properly fed and watered faerie snit could grow into an all-out war.

That Delta seemed wary about moving forward gave me the internal giggles. We all have our base level of normal. Mine leaned way over the line of wonky. She fights magical entities gone wrong, all I do is keep the peace between my godmothers.

Circling left, we passed through a stone arch

leading into a courtyard right out of a romantic fantasy. An oasis of summer on the edge of a winter day.

A centrally located fountain pitched colored water in the air to splash down in a circular basin of purest white marble shot through with gold veins. A riot of flowers bloomed, all of them out of season, to soothe the senses and entice the nose with glorious scents.

"Give me a tent in the corner," Delta offered, "I think I've found my new home."

"Too bad it's a castle that comes complete with a full set of drama queens." I pointed toward the cluster of furious faeries and willful witches. "Peace is rarely on the menu, and when it is, you savor it. Don't get me wrong, I love them all, and I wouldn't change a thing." Most of the time, anyway. It would have been nice to live out my childhood fantasies for an hour or so before magical Armageddon raged.

"Drama queens. I see what you did there. Want me to handle this one?"

I almost did, just to see if I could pick up any pointers. I suspected Delta had game. As it happened, neither one of us needed to step in. The fight ended when Terra caught sight of us watching.

"Can it! Lexi's here," she hissed at the others, and all six of them turned sympathetic faces my way. It was all head tilts and conciliatory nods these days.

I'd rather have them fighting than feeling sorry for me. "What do you think? It's pretty, right?" They'd done this for me. Love for my ragtag family blew through me. I should have known a fairytale castle wasn't Mag's style or Clara's either.

Still, castles and princesses tend to lead one toward thoughts of handsome princes, and since I'd recently lost mine, the joy from the chance at living out a childhood fantasy popped like a balloon blown up too fast. I think I even heard the *pffft* noise in the back of my head.

"It is. You'll all remember Delta, she's staying the night." I put the castle behind me and made my way back to the kitchen. I felt the magic swell, then dissipate behind me as each faerie withdrew the elements they'd used in the building process. I didn't need to watch to know the earth tidied itself behind the stone walls as they sank below the surface.

"Buzzkill," Delta spoke the absolute truth, and I didn't care. Pain had become my constant companion, and even if it was tinged with hope at times, at others, it rolled over me like a wave, dashed my heart on the rocks with its undertow.

We stopped long enough to pile a tray with food—I'm an emotional eater—and I led the way upstairs. Maybe Delta's story would take my mind off other things. We settled on the bed, trusted Terra's nifty little clean-up spell to take care of crumbs, and Delta launched into her tale between bites.

"This is scratch-made bread, isn't it? And freshly churned butter. Do you know I could make a meal out of this just by itself? Anyway, what do you know about the history of Fate Weavers?"

"About enough to fill a baby's dimple and still leave room to decorate."

"Okay. You know Eros—Cupid, I think you call him—has always been a bit of a..." Delta paused, I could only assume, to search for a word that wouldn't offend.

"You can say it. He was a horndog. Jett tossed that in my face the first time we met." Not that I had any major feelings about my father in that sense. How was I supposed to get offended on his behalf when I'd never even met the man?

"It's not just him, but I'm not going to spread gossip. Anyway, given that his source of power lay in the romantic realm, your father cut quite a swath through the world, and then he got tangled up with a woman who had been blessed by Hecate."

"A witch," I pointed out to show I was following along with the story.

She reached for a third slice of bread and slathered it with softened butter. "Yes, and not just any witch, but one with a great deal of powerful magic and a hunger for more. The stars blazed in the sky the night they consummated the relationship and Eros planted his seed. Magics mixed and melded to create a child like no other that had come before."

It all had a fairytale ring to it, but I was still waiting

on her to cue the villain of the piece.

"A Fate Weaver. Interesting story, but I already know about the genetics."

"I can stop if you don't want to hear the rest." Delta swung off the bed, put her empty plate on my desk, and began to stalk around the room with the lithe grace of a panther.

"Sorry. I want to hear. I really do." What little information I had about my heritage was half speculation and the rest inferred from the cryptic comments my grandmother and aunt occasionally exchanged. "I'll shut up now, I promise."

"What do you know about karma?" Seemed like an odd change of subject and a stupid question.

"I'm a witch, we may not call it karma, but we know all about the rule of threes and the soul debt that comes with having enough power to inflict our intentions on the world. Payback is a witch, right?"

"That's not the way I heard it, but close enough. Anyway, where I'm from, they laugh at the idea of karma. It's just not a thing they have to worry about. They do as they please and use the human world as a convenient gauge for keeping track of the results; making sure they don't inadvertently bring about the end of the universe."

"Which makes us what—a cross between a thermometer and pawns on a game board?" Excuse me if that sounded bitter.

"You play chess?" Delta pulled the chair from my desk, turned it, so the back faced me, and settled down in a straddled position.

"Faerie chess, but I'm not sure it counts as the real thing because the rules are different."

"Faerie chess?"

I explained how the love of board games turned game nights into epic events when my godmothers were involved. They tended to mix and match games to suit their whims, and then we played them out in life-sized venues. Faerie chess had all the same pieces as the standard version, and the endgame was the same—capture the queen—but the rest of the rules differed wildly. Think checkers meets backgammon and toss in a dash of Monopoly for good measure.

"Stop. Don't tell me any more, you're making my brain hurt, and I can see this was a faulty analogy. What I'm getting at is there's a duality in the universe that needs to be preserved. Yin and Yang. Day and night. Up and down. Everything has an opposite."

"Good and evil? I'm aware of the concept." It was one I contemplated from time to time; mostly when confronted by the flip side of love. I circled a hand to indicate she should continue.

"Then you'll understand what I mean when I say your world is not some kind of game board, it's the fulcrum point of the universe. If it tips into the darkness, all the worlds will follow."

"Oh, so no pressure, then." Sarcasm happens when I find a concept uncomfortable to process. "What does all this have to do with the first Fate Weaver?"

"I'm getting to that. I assume you had heard of Cupid before you discovered the family connection." I nodded. "Well, he earned his reputation for being a bed-hopping love-them-and-leave-them type until he hooked up with the witch and on the day the first Fate Weaver was born, the old boy got a bit of a shock."

Since I'd gone back in time to another moment when my father had been taken aback, I had an idea what his surprised face looked like. It helped me get a visual as the story progressed.

"A piece of the baby's humanity took up residence in your father's soul. He got a taste of what it meant to be touched by karma and it had a powerful effect on him. Making matches suddenly turned into serious work, and when he started putting more thought and effort behind the job, others took notice."

"What does all this have to do with me," I asked. I'd been hoping to learn the greater purpose behind making matches. Seemed like Delta expected me to pull some nugget of truth out of her story that I just wasn't seeing.

Delta sighed loudly and explained. "With every new Fate Weaver, the stain of humanity welled inside him, and his reaction was to make more matches. True love, kiss and all, grew out of his tainted soul."

"You say this like it's a bad thing." Outrage forced

the words from me. "True love is what I'm all about. It's what drives me, what drives the world. It's beautiful and good. How can that be a bad thing?"

Again, she looked at me like I was too simple to understand the concept. "Where the other gods watched from the outside, Cupid stepped in and created a shift in the duality. He meddled in people's fates and even though his intentions were good, his actions had to be balanced by the creation of opposing forces and now the human heart has become more than just a pivot point, it's a battleground."

I think I got it now. "You're saying my father is at the heart of all the nasty things humans do to each other. He poked his finger into our love lives and stirred up a hornet's nest of reciprocal pain."

"I'm not saying that at all. Love has softened many a warring heart, but it drives them, too. Along with loving comes fighting, and those who would unmake the universe figured that fact out quickly and perverted love to suit their own dark desires. The dichotomy evolved until you, and those like you became more important than ever."

Pat Benatar's voice echoed through my head.

"Love really is a battlefield." The Bow of Destiny chimed in with a convincing guitar lick. I smiled.

"It is now, and not only because Fate Weavers came to be, but also because they instinctively picked up the gauntlet and ran into the fray. You made matches long before you knew it was in your blood to do so. When Cupid set the ball in motion, he had no idea it would turn into a behemoth and roll over him as well as the family he was so keen to perpetuate."

I felt, well, my emotions were so mixed up I wasn't sure what I felt, so I fell silent for a moment and tuned in to sort them out.

There was pride in providing a measure of protection to the world, chagrin for not having taken my job seriously enough. Trepidation because my very existence made me a target—and now some of my grandmother's mutterings made sense—and over it all, a fierce sense of purpose. Plus a measure of annoyance that my father had been the architect of change that could make or break the world.

I hadn't been the one to set events in motion, but as a child of Cupid, as a Fate Weaver, and don't forget I'm a Balefire, one of the most powerful witches of my generation, I would do my part going forward. You know…once I knew exactly what my part entailed. The rock ballad in my head changed to a stirring march.

"Lexi, you realize this makes you a…"

"…Target. Yeah, I got that already. For every action, there is an opposite and equal reaction. My fourth-grade teacher was fond of saying something like that. I have enemies, my matches are more important than I realized. I'm up to speed." A mental image of my current nemesis rose in my head. "What can you tell me about Diana Diamond?"

"Ah, that one. She's trouble."

"Yeah, that I knew. I need more."

"Granddaughter of Psyche. Born into a Romany line known to be endowed with a strong level of psychic ability. Carries a deck of cards that…you know it would be easier just to show you."

Delta reached into a concealed pocket, pulled out a shiny, metallic stone and tossed it to me. Instinct guided my hand in snatching the rock from the air, and when it made contact, the vision rolled over me.

Chapter 15

"Try this one." An apple-cheeked woman brushed a ripple of raven curls behind one ear and handed a deck of cards to a girl with the face of an angel while I watched from above. The vision felt full of import and breathless anticipation. "Do the cards speak to you, little one?"

"The pictures are pretty, and I like the colors." Eager to please, small fingers leafed through the Bosch Tarot, laid one card after another face up on the table. Like a series of old masters, each card of the Bosch deck had a painterly feel to it. Fine art.

"But do they speak? Do you feel them in your bones?"

"No, I don't think so."

"And these?" A Ryder deck replaced the Bosch, and I angled in for a closer look at the girl's face. A young Diana concentrated, trying almost too hard to feel something and please the woman who patiently watched.

"I'm sorry, Yaya. I'm trying very hard."

Mist washed the tableau away, replaced it with another. Older now, Diana opened brightly painted doors, furtively searched through the contents of a set of cabinets. Every so often, she glanced over one shoulder to make sure she was alone.

Pulling a velvet bag with a drawstring closure from the inky depths, she returned to the table and dumped the contents into her hand. Runestones, polished by years of handling, bright with color, trickled across her palm to spill on the velvet cloth. After playing with them for a few minutes, Diana lost interest and returned to the cabinet to root around for another treasure.

A carved wooden box yielded bones, smoothed to an ivory shine. Those held less appeal than the runes, and within minutes lay scattered on the table, abandoned.

Back to the cupboards she went and threw open another door to rifle through the contents. Reaching into the farthest corner, she pulled out a parcel wrapped in soft black cloth and tied with a series of intricate knots. Her breath caught and so did mine as some powerful magic made itself known. The kind that sets the tiny bones in your ears to humming and vibrates the back of your tongue until you feel it in your throat.

Sweeping aside the runes and bones, Diana lay the bundle on the table and poked at the knots with a gentle fingertip. I sensed anticipation tinged with wariness rising in the girl, but no hint of what I knew she would someday become.

At her touch, the knots magically fell away. Wild magic rode a set of blank cards that lay on the table waiting to be touched and tamed and used for good or evil. The cards cared little for the purpose, only for the act of being played.

Diana reached for the one on top, and without thinking too hard about it, I surged forward and laid an astral finger on the deck at the same time she touched it. The colorful image of the Fool formed, but whatever Diana saw or felt with that first touch, I never knew because I had been sucked into another place and time.

Two women—sister goddesses, given the resemblance between them and the level of power they commanded—faced each other across a slab of gold-veined marble with a polished sheen.

"It's your turn to deal, Aneris." One sister slid a deck of cards across the table.

Picking up the deck, Aneris said, "Dealer's choice and I choose War." I knew the game, I'd played it with Terra once upon a time.

The first sister grumbled. "I hate that game."

"Too bad, Eris, you made the rules. Dealer's choice." And the game was on.

I felt right at home watching Aneris and Eris squabble, though when the faeries fight, they don't have the power to make and unmake destinies, so that's a relief. You always think your situation is the worst and it never is.

The trouble was, this game played out on the field of man. Now I knew where our history of going to war began.

Each slap of the cards on the stone table sent another shockwave of war across the world until mighty Zeus seemed to have had enough. Eris pulled a king to cover Aneris' nine of spades, but before she could play it, a bolt of lightning hit the center of the table and the game vanished in a cloud of ozone-scented air. The blast sent both sisters sprawling.

Winged shoes hovering a few inches above the floor, Hermes appeared and said, "There was a consensus, and we've decided you've done enough damage with these." He brandished the deck of cards. "I'll be putting them someplace safe from the pair of you, and you're not to go looking for them."

The cards wrapped themselves in soft cloth, tied with twine, and Hermes dropped the familiar-looking bundle into a pouch he carried at his waist—the elevated version of a fanny pack. I imagined him bouncing down a runway in his flapping shoes and executing a flawless hip-shot model turn just for fun. Olympus faded to black, and then the vision opened again on an aerial view of a Romany Vardo wagon nestled in the corner of a small field.

Hermes skimmed over the arched roof and came to a running stop just behind the rustic home decorated with brightly-painted scrolls and flower patterns around the windows and doors. A white goat pranced over to test his hand for edibles, and finding none, gave Hermes a friendly, but firm head-butt.

"Hello, the house!" He called out and circled to put a foot on the first step.

The top half of a Dutch door swung open, and a woman scowled through the opening. "I'm not going back, and I won't let you take my Diana."

"I didn't come here to take you or your daughter anywhere, Bianca." At his assurance, Bianca's attitude underwent a subtle change; she relaxed and turned on the charm.

"Well then, why don't you come inside, I'm sure we can find something that will make your trip worth the time." Bianca arched her back, displayed her wares while her eyes raked over the tight-fitting leggings to linger on the part of his anatomy she found most interesting.

Heated blood rose to stain Hermes' face, and Bianca quirked a smile at the sight of the dull red skin.

"I've just come to give you this, and it comes with a message from your mother."

The smile fell off Bianca's face, but she took the parcel he offered.

"Psyche asked me to give you her love and to tell

you she trusts you to keep this safe."

Another woman, even another daughter of a living Goddess might have torn away the wrappings to see what was inside. Made of sterner stuff, Bianca turned and stowed the deck of cards in the back of the nearest cabinet. The action gave her time to compose her features.

"Is that all? She didn't send a message to Diana?"

Hermes shrugged and turned away as the vision within a vision faded.

In her next incarnation, Diana Diamond, poised on the brink of leaving adolescence, danced with a beautiful, raven-haired boy with an innocent face and a gentle smile. Love shone in the brightness of her eyes as he graced her with the shyest of kisses. The tender moment evoked the memory of my first kiss. All the wonder and flutter and thunder of hearts as his lips met mine. I sighed. Anyone would.

While Diana fell headlong into young love, she used the stolen, goddess-touched Tarot cards to tell fortune after fortune with unparalleled accuracy. Folks came from miles around to hear their futures and her star continued to rise.

Perhaps her young man feared what she might learn about him, for even the most shining youth has a shadowed side. But over time, another pretty lass caught his eye, one with simpler tastes. The callow boy could not find the words to let Diana down easy, so he said nothing at all.

He loves me, he loves me not, Diana asked herself until the question was too hard to bear, so she pulled out the cards that had served her so well and did the unthinkable: she laid out a spread to tell her own future.

The future is not set in stone—Gran jokes that her past once was, but that's a different concept altogether—and no matter how good the telling, your fortune can change in an instant. Diana had come to think herself so infallible a prophet she was capable of predicting her own future.

Whatever Diana saw turned her cold and hard as her namesake, she embraced the raw power, craved more, and burned her world to ashes. The cards absorbed every ounce of magic she poured into them, begged for more until, with a wicked smile on her face, she pulled out a penknife.

The knife flashed silver when it scored the palm of her left hand, blood gathered like a row of scarlet beads along the shallow line. Darkness writhed as though it lived and breathed and waited for the moment that comes just before a soul takes its plunge—when everything is balanced on the edge.

Triumphant, Diana squeezed her fist, held it high, and let the first drop fall.

A sizzle at the point of impact, a tiny puff of smoke, and then a shrieking whirlwind of power tore Diana into little pieces that rode the tornado for a moment before coming back together again minus one very important part. Diana's heart, her emotional center, held no light, no love. It was as black and dark as a moonless night.

Dark heart. The term bounced around in my head the way a song does when it's become an earworm that just won't stop repeating. Dark heart.

Darkest Heart.

In case you were wondering, slapping your forehead in astral form hurts just the same as in the physical. I remembered hearing a story about the darkest heart when the earthbound angel Adriel and the faerie godmothers teamed up to release Vaeta from the underworld.

If Diana was the Darkest Heart, she was more of an enemy than I'd bargained for. Not just a rival matchmaker, not just the bearer of a magical deck of Tarot cards powerful enough to override true love's kiss, Diana Diamond was the granddaughter of Psyche herself. That gave her what—a quarter share of a blood tie to a mythic Goddess?

A share, from what I'd seen, she'd been willing to do anything to strengthen. Bianca might not have wanted to embrace her heritage, but she'd raised a daughter who was only too happy to trade on the power of Olympus.

Most people have an annoying neighbor for a worst enemy, but I get a slew of heartless, ticked off godlings who would like nothing more than to burn the world down and blow on the ashes. How did I get to be the one elected to fix this?

Oh, that's right. My father and his need to experience the human condition. Thanks, Dad.

If I thought I'd seen all I needed to see, the director behind this little montage wasn't quite finished. The finale saw me back in my own body observing the cute couple I'd matched with the elevated fates.

I found myself watching them, their heads huddled together over a table in a restaurant across town, and I wasn't alone. Diana Diamond had joined me in the vision or astral projection or whatever the technical term was for what was happening.

Judging by the look on her face as she stood across from me, she'd tuned into the intensity of their emotions as well. Her face was…um…not her face.

Getting a peek under the mask proved Delta's vision true; Diana was a powerful demigod and not the kind born of love or light or laughter, but a goddess of darkness and pain and infinite unhappiness.

Endless shadows played peek-a-boo with her features, shifting to give me a glimpse of eyes burning black over lips pressed into a tight line of displeasure that bordered on pain. Focused on the couple, she gave no indication she was aware of my presence as the shadows shifted and obscured her face again.

When a flare of pink drew my attention to the table

and joy flooded over me, I forgot all about Diana. The sensation was so pure it played on my tattered, lovesick emotions and tweaked them to the point of pain.

"This is…I can't…I have to kiss you right now, or I think I might die." He leaned in close, gave her a chance to turn away, but she bridged the gap and breathed into the kiss. Lips met softly, made promises without words, parted slightly then dived in again. A kiss to bind them for eternity—one that stole my breath away as theirs quickened with desire. Time stood still for a split second, then I felt the rumble of it starting back up again.

And more, I felt hearts lift and sing in a world a little brighter than it had been before.

Behold the power of love to beat back all that would seek to play one human against another until darkness overbalanced the light.

The thing that was Diana's true self howled behind its shadow mask; a sound of frustration and fury and pain so intense I almost felt sorry for it, for her. Almost.

It's not the absence of pain that marks a person as true of heart. Wickedness, as I've come to learn, lies in the choices we make when faced with despair. Witches and gods might have more power than humans, but free will is the real battleground.

The vision popped like a bubble.

"And she's back." Delta juggled three knives, blades flashing in a mesmerizing arc. "What?" She said when she caught me staring. "I was bored."

"Most people just read a magazine."

"Most people would ask what you just saw."

Looked like Delta wasn't so different as she thought.

I described the visions, asked a few questions to which Delta had no answers until her head perked up, and she cut me off mid-sentence.

"Business. Gotta bail. Back when I can." A whirl of black leather and she was gone.

Chapter 16

It irritated me to no end that Delta just up and disappeared, once again leaving me with a myriad of questions and fewer answers than I'd have liked. For one thing, how had Diana gotten her true nature past me? A shield that strong was a handy trick to have up your sleeve, and one I'd make good use of myself.

It was almost enough to make me forget about my own personal love issues. For just a few moments the pain, as it sometimes does in these situations, gave way to a pleasant numbness.

The only problem was, while I was rolling around and reveling in its absence, the pain came crushing back to pull me further into its undertow. I pushed those feelings back and found enough calm to focus on figuring out my next step, and what my gut told me was that I might not have to look further than inside myself for the answers to my questions.

Blessedly, the house had gone silent when I padded back downstairs, and I spared no precious seconds wondering what aligning of the stars had transpired to empty the place precisely when I needed no distraction.

In the sanctum, I found a quiet corner I'd never seen before, lined with embroidered silk pillows and festooned with a canopy of chiffon from floor to ceiling. A perfect spot for meditation, the room knew exactly what I'd needed and offered it willingly. Being a witch? Coolest thing ever.

I settled cross-legged into the cushions and reached behind my head to grasp one of the arrows from the invisible quiver slung across my back. I rolled it between my fingers and brushed the pad of my thumb against the shaft. When I'd picked up the bow for the first time and realized I was missing its quintessential counterpart I thought for a split second my search for and repair of the instrument had all been for nothing.

Imagine my surprise when I was able to pull a living gold-tipped arrow out of *myself*. It felt like the shaft was made of my own bones, and I couldn't even begin to discern what type of otherworldly bird had supplied the fletching feathers.

Regardless, each time I'd seen the goddess had corresponded to the nocking of said arrows, so I fitted the one in my hand to string and hoped she wouldn't disappoint me now, when I needed her more than ever.

Mercifully, the goddess shivered into being in front of me, mimicking my pose but without the hunched shoulders and maudlin expression. Her back was ramrod straight, each one of her pink-tipped blond hairs in perfect place, no tear-stained cheeks or raccoon eyes.

"It's about time you decided to address me directly." Shocking me, she spoke in a clear, articulate voice I wished was mine but knew from hearing myself on Terra's home movies that it certainly wasn't. "I'm getting bored in here; what's the holdup?" Well, the attitude was definitely mine.

"I'm sorry you're bored?" It came out more like a question than an apology, and my cheeks pinked in mortification. Could I be any lamer?

"We have enemies bearing down on us, and you've just been sitting around with your arrows up your ass letting it happen. We have a job to do; let's get on with it!"

Yep, definitely my attitude.

"So how do we break Diana Diamond's hold on Kin? How do we fix this?"

"Kin is just a distraction, the stakes are higher than that. Do you remember that couple from the street? I know you felt a greater purpose behind that match; a heightened sense of accomplishment, and the pushback from another force."

I nodded, "Kin is more to me than just a distraction, but yes, of course, I remember."

"We mated two souls that day—two souls our new nemesis didn't want to be matched. Why do you think that is?"

I'd been contemplating the same question ever since I learned it was Diana Diamond's wrath I'd felt that day, and the only answer I could come up with is that the pair was some sort of linchpin in the cosmic machine.

As if she read my mind, she answered, "Yes, exactly, you're on the right track. You know what your problem is?" My goddess stopped and stared at me. Apparently, it was necessary for me to ask the stupid question.

"No, what?"

"You don't trust your instincts, and you keep trying to make sense of something that defies human logic."

Trust my instincts? Last time I did that, I got hoodwinked by my own mother. Talk about once burned, twice shy. "Well maybe if anyone ever thought to tell me anything, I'd know what the heck I'm supposed to be doing!"

"That's a lame excuse you use when life gets tough, and now you're using it to avoid taking control of your destiny. Answer the call when it comes, don't be a total idiot."

"You mean that annoying music the stupid bow is always playing?"

"Yes, that stupid bow that opens hearts and fortifies

love. You think you have enemies coming out of the woodwork and that you're the focus of their hatred, but you're not. Human hearts are the battlefield, and right now we're not the only ones wrestling for control. Not everything in the world is about you, Lexi Balefire."

No kidding. Who did she think I was, anyway? Some egotistical brat? Okay, maybe I was sometimes, but really, isn't everyone at times?

"And what about the rest of the world? Port Harbor is just one tiny town. Or are we living on some Hellmouth I don't know about?"

She blew out a sigh. "This isn't Sunnydale, smarty pants. But power attracts power, and we have a lot at our disposal. Or at least, we would if you suck it up, put on your big girl undies, and start doing your job. You saw what complacency leads to—do you want to be responsible for that?"

"Of course not. But what about Kin? Am I just supposed to give up on him?"

Goddess Lexi rolled her eyes and raised one eyebrow in a gesture so full of contempt I vowed to nix it from my own repertoire. If that old urban legend about your face getting stuck in one expression ever comes true, I don't want to spend eternity looking bitchy.

"No, dummy. Can't you see how screwing with the love life of the most powerful Fate Weaver ever born might be a good distraction? Obviously, your relationship with Kin is important—but you can't lose sight of the greater good while you throw the world's most pathetic pity party. Trace the problem back to the source."

"Oh." Stellar comeback.

One final pointed look, and I was alone in the room once more. Unless you count a whole host of heavy new thoughts, anyway.

Chapter 17

After everything I'd seen and heard, the cell phone jingling from my pocket suddenly seemed alien and inconsequential. I checked the screen, saw Serena's number, and, vowing to call her back as soon as I had the opportunity, clicked ignore.

The Bow of Destiny had been blatting in my ear ever since, or maybe because Delta's vision gift had come to an end, and no matter how vehemently I pleaded for a decrease in volume, it just got louder and louder until I had no choice but to submit and follow its pull. If the thing was this insistent, whoever required my services must be in dire need.

I straddled Bluebell thinking for the first time that maybe Flix was right and I should upgrade to a bigger bike. Maybe connecting to my innate power had also connected me more solidly to the earth's energy, because that ride through the countryside with Delta had been more exhilarating than any night I'd ever spent on the streets of Port Harbor.

Don't get me wrong, I'm not about to buy myself a pair of hiking boots and a bird watching handbook or anything, but the clean, fresh country air had cleared the cobwebs from my brain, and I wouldn't say no to a repeat performance.

For now, I found myself being drawn to one of the city's main attractions—a mile-long strip of scenic views wending from the northern edge of the historic district, along the banks of the Piscatakeag River, to a boardwalk overlooking the Port Harbor estuary. Late November wind cut through my insufficient denim jacket, its bite stinging ever colder as I drove into the frigid ocean breeze.

Not many days left before snow forced Bluebell into her winter cocoon.

After stashing the scooter beneath a flickering street lamp, I hurried along, guided by the bow's eardrum-popping volume and the pull in my belly. Ahead of me on the boardwalk, a potential couple stood out from the crowd. Or rather the disparate parts of a potential couple. Amid a chattering group waiting in line for a table at Banmai's, I spotted a flutter of pink hovering in the air.

Nice, this would be an easy one. Fire an arrow, bing bang boom, done and dusted.

The cheery pink hearts signaled my quarry, and I

was halfway toward calling up the carrier of the bow when I realized the symbol over the man's head was black, and the pink one hovered over another guy's head. Worse, Diana Diamond was bearing down from the opposite direction.

It appeared that destiny expected me to solidify some fates before she had the chance to interfere.

I didn't need Captain Obvious to show up and dance around shouting the shiny pink guy was the better choice, but I took half a second to tune into Mr. Blackheart just to see what I could learn.

Nothing evil about him, just wrong for her—as if this woman choosing that man would lead to unhappiness and pain. Diana had already—possibly—doomed Kin and me to a similar fate, and if there was a way for me to prevent her from connecting with her next target, I'd do whatever it took.

I made a move to reach for my weapon and nearly fell over when my new nemesis showed me her true form. I'd seen it before, but now Diana looked even scarier than she had before. High cheekbones slashed like razors beneath piercing dark eyes and a wicked smirk twisted blood-red lips. Dusky veins traced a pattern below the surface of skin so pale it was nearly translucent. Dark power encased her like a shroud.

I shivered.

She flicked fingers tipped with wickedly sharp nails painted to match her lips and drew a card from beneath her cloak. Bow song jangled in my head and the urge to shoot an arrow brought the goddess out with a rush of warrior energy that fired me up, too.

Diana—or that thing that had been Diana, once upon a time—faced me from the opposite side of the three targets as though we were two gunslingers in an old western movie. We both moved at the same time: me with my heart-tipped arrow promising a life filled with love and contentment; and she with her evil-infused square of goddess magic carrying heartache and suffering.

In a rush of stomach-lurching speed, both card and arrow hurtled toward the woman and before I had time to process what had happened a shimmering version of Diana's card rose to hover over the newly made couple like a map marker set squarely in the middle of a ring of seething shadow.

Dread stole into my throat, lodged there like a lump as my arrow bounced off the woman's chest, fell to the ground, and dissipated with a hiss in a puff of swirling ether. She'd won and I had failed.

Time all but stopped for the next minute. Diana's doing, I could only assume.

Sauntering unseen toward the newly made couple, Diana swiped her index finger through the black mist, captured a tiny bit of ebony on the tip, and in a manner I can only describe as sensual, slid the darkness between hungry lips to sample the flavor.

Ick. The heebies took it up to the level of skin-crawling disgust. And then, it got worse.

Hungry noises growled in Diana's throat as she leaned forward and slurped up the inky pool. A slimy drop decorated her full bottom lip when she turned back toward me.

Her eyes were black with hate and fury and pure evil. Dark, ropy veins rose to the surface of her skin, pulsed and writhed like snakes as she became more…I wasn't sure what she was becoming, actually. A demon? Something else? Whatever it was couldn't be good, not with the way the mere vision of her chilled me to the bone.

Diana turned, let out a satisfied laugh, looked me square in the eye, raised her eyebrow in a silent challenge, and then disappeared as swiftly as my arrow had only moments before.

As much as I wanted to hate her, there was a part of me that understood how easy it had been for Diana to turn to the dark side. If it wasn't for my Cupid-bestowed affinity for lovers—and the unwavering hope that accompanied it like the free sample of conditioner plexi-wrapped to bottles of shampoo—the loss of Kin might have had a similar effect on my psyche.

Left without hope, I might have allowed myself to fall into the deep well of wickedness or maybe let the goddess take my soul to a place where the pain no longer burned.

My shoulders slumped with the weight of epic failure, but as I turned to leave, I noticed the card Diana had flung, lying on the ground where the newly-formed couple had been.

Touching it held about as much appeal as poking a ticked-off snake with my finger, but I felt compelled to pick it up. The second my finger met the surface I knew I should have listened to my common sense.

Black mist billowed out of the card and spread over me like a cloud. When it cleared, I found my astral self standing in front of a wall-sized map pinned with nearly an entire deck similar to the one I now held. The center of each one was marked with a damp and darkened ring, and there were enough of them that it looked like she'd spread her hatred over a significant part of the world. Was that her goal? To blanket the world in a morass of discontent?

Was it some kind of cry for help or evidence of her inability to handle misery alone? A tiny part of me felt sorry for her, but not enough to show up at her office with wine and share a chick power moment.

Thankfully, I was in my own body this time—or at least a representation of it. Conjuring a bit of witchlight to augment and provide clarity, I watched the suits quiver and shift. Black diamonds, red spades, clubs turned to hearts in a blur of motion.

Before I had time to wonder what it all meant, Diana stepped into the room wearing her everyday face and carrying another card in her hand. The four of cups landed in the middle of the tabletop.

In the mythic deck, the suit of cups told a story of Psyche's relationship with Eros. The four depicted the moment when Psyche's step-sisters used gossip and innuendo to send her down the wrong path in her marriage to Eros.

Eros. Cupid by another name. Dad seemed to be tied to everything annoying in my life lately.

The card represented a crossroads and the beginning of a betrayal. Eros had asked one thing of his new wife: that she never look upon his face. If she could do this one thing, their marriage would be happy and prosperous. In the blush of love, Psyche agreed until her meddling step-sisters filled her head with doubts and the temptation to look upon the face of her true love.

Overcome with an uncontrollable desire to do the one thing she shouldn't, Psyche waited until Eros went to sleep and then took a peek thinking he'd never know the difference. She could not have been more wrong. Eros woke up, saw that his wife had betrayed his trust and walked away without a backward glance, leaving Psyche alone and scorned.

My dad. Good at cutting people out of his life. Just ask my half-brother who blamed me when it happened to his mother.

Family angst went out of my head when the vision sped up so fast it reminded me of those IMAX short movies with the roller coaster point of view. It is possible to suffer motion sickness when you are standing still. Crazy world

The next thing I knew, I was inside Diana's skin. Again. This vision thing had once seemed like a blessing, I was beginning to rethink my position on that.

From her point of view, I watched our recent skirmish play out, the missile of her will flickering in her hand just before she winged it. I felt her greed, hate, passion, and under it all, pain. Oh, I might be well on my way to hating her with every fiber of my being, but I understood Diana better than she would ever understand me.

When I realized she was about to suck in the black aura of her misdeeds, I fought like a hellcat for release.

I won't go into detail about the taste of darkness, other than to say it's bitter and somehow seductive. When Diana turned away, my astral self stepped free and I noticed a card lying on the ground.

A Queen of diamonds. Appropriate given the name of the evil thing who'd thrown it, I suppose. As if being directed by something larger or more knowing, I felt compelled to step closer and saw the smiling Queen's face flicker and shift. How odd.

Deliberately, I let my eyes go unfocused until I could make out red diamonds rapidly turning to black hearts. The Queen's smile changed, too. From an enigmatic twist of the lips to something sinister and knowing.

Queen of the black hearts. Black hearts, the symbols of Diana's dark will.

I knew there was more to learn if I was brave enough to stay and wait until I'd seen it all. No part of me wanted to be that brave, and still, I stayed and watched.

Time twisted back on itself as my failure played out in reverse, then froze again at the moment the card lanced Ms. Pink Heart's skin. This was my chance to see what else I could glean, so I stepped forward, laid a hand tentatively on the woman's back, and let her future slide through me.

An unhappy marriage had not been Diana's goal, or if it was, she'd missed the mark. Unless this woman's misery hadn't been the primary target. Circling the tableau, I tested the man who should have been matched and promptly forgot to breathe.

Dark images. Darker emotions. Scorned men and women turning from love, this man among them. Turning hard like Diana. An army spewing hate into the world and painting it with the black pain of betrayal. Inch by inch, the wave of discontent spread across the world.

Like a news report from hell, a reel of destruction played out for me. Building hurt and hate until the final death of love created the dark world Diana craved. Card after card lanced the hearts of her intended victims;

Diana had been at this a long time, and I was late to the party.

The vision shifted from history through the present and into the future until the final card spun into an innocent heart and I saw what Diana had been working to accomplish. When the last, card-borne death of love fed the darkness of her heart, the dark Goddess devoured the final shred of her own humanity and Diana ascended to god status.

As if she'd known I was watching all along, the evil thing laughed and the sharp sound of it cut the vision to shreds all around me.

I can't tell you how I got home, only that I was on autopilot the whole way.

Chapter 18

"Why do you think hanging around with that beanpole is a good idea?" Whenever Flix mentioned Serena, his nose wrinkled with distaste and not in a manly way, either. I wasn't sure why he was so focused on her lately, but he couldn't stop complaining about her.

"That beanpole is about to become family. I've made up with her, and you might try opening yourself up and having a little empathy, considering that's what you supposedly do best. Serena did some unspeakable things, but if I can give her a second chance, so can you. She called and asked if she could come over, that's a huge step for her considering our history, and I'm sure it wasn't easy. I'm not asking you to be friends with her, just don't be mean. Okay?"

"Fine. But only because you're my best friend. Otherwise, I'd let that witch rot."

I didn't believe it for a second; Flix has a heart of gold, it's just buried under fifteen layers of snark. Riding solo for a couple of weeks while Carl went to some remote location I couldn't remember the name of, to study something else I also couldn't recall, Flix had fallen into his old habit of showing up at my house unannounced.

It felt like the old days, which made me sad for some reason.

"I'll admit she has the worst taste in men, and I've pointed that out to her enough that she's been avoiding me for the past few days, but it doesn't take an empath to know she's scared."

Not that she'd sounded scared when she called. Furious was more like it and probably with me because that was the fallback position in our relationship. "Honestly, this is the worst time for her to show up here. Right when I'm trying to figure out how to deal with Diana Diamond."

Flix wanted to know what I was up against, so I described my visions of her to him using as few words as possible.

"Got it. Crazy wannabe Goddess uses enchanted Tarot cards to increase her power base while subverting true love because she traded her heart for the chance to evolve. For the love of Danu, Lexi. You sure know how to pick them."

Don't I know it.

"I was the pickee, not the picker in this case. It's a Fate Weaver thing according to Delta. I'm glad she showed up, or I'd be flying mostly blind. I'm beginning to think there's a conspiracy to keep me from learning the things I need to know."

"Then why didn't you bother asking us?" My entire household stepped through the sanctum door, filing in one by one; faerie, witch, familiar, alternating down the line.

"Salem, I swear to the goddess, you're in for a lifelong kitty kibble sentence for tattling. I told you I needed time to think this problem through on my own." I shot daggers at him from my position in the center of the casting circle.

"Technically speaking I didn't break any rules." Salem's eyes shifted over to the faeries, "they wrestled it out of me."

"They couldn't have done that if you weren't playing along, and we all know it."

"You should have talked to us yourself, Lexi," Gran stepped forward, "I know you're trying to be strong, and keep everyone safe, but you're putting yourself at risk and if anything were to happen to *you*, and *we* could have prevented it, we'd never forgive ourselves."

A little piece of me, one I suspected came directly from my mother, mounted a silent protest. When would they ever think I was strong enough to fill out my witch shoes like a big girl? According to Delta, I was the most powerful Fate Weaver my father ever made, so where was the respect?

Rhetorical questions since it wasn't about respect or recognizing my strength; the protectiveness came from their love for me and nowhere else. Only the most ungrateful wretch on the planet would react to care and affection with churlish behavior, so I stuffed my ego back in its cave and laid out what I knew for the group.

"Serena's on her way, and I was just talking Flix out of sniping at her, she sounded scared enough as it is." Six months ago, if you'd told me I would defend this woman to anyone, I would have called you something unflattering before dissolving into a puddle of uncontrollable giggles, but I wasn't laughing now.

Under the top layer of ticked off, I'd heard a tremor of fear in Serena's voice and the words she'd left unsaid tangled my guts into a knot of worry.

Worse, I was missing huge chunks of a conversation I really wanted to hear. Go figure, the first time anyone wanted to fill me in on bits of lore that applied directly to my heritage and I couldn't focus.

As the minutes passed, I couldn't shake the sudden conviction she might not make it here at all until finally, my nerves triggered an adrenaline boost, and I knew I had to do something.

"I have to…" Concentrating on Serena's face, I focused hard so my will would take me to her. My skimming technique was still a work in progress. As it turned out, I didn't have to go far and shimmered back into my skin at the end of the block.

"Oh. My. Goddess." When I caught sight of her form, bowed around a belly heavier with child than any I'd ever seen, I nearly fell over. In the span of two weeks, she'd gone from sporting an easily camouflaged baby bump to the waddling form of a full-term pregnancy. Not normal.

"What did you…? How did that…? Let me help you." I slung an arm around her for support and guided her closer to the safety of the Balefire house. "You should have said something, I would have sent Gran to you."

Serena winced, either in pain or annoyance. "She wouldn't have been safe. I might have doomed you all by coming here, but I didn't know where else to go. It's Jett. He did this to me, and I've only just managed to get away from him."

A touch of our prior relationship reared its ugly head when she added, "No thanks to you, you self-centered jerk. I know you were dodging my calls."

For once, I let the insult go. Look at me showing personal growth. It wasn't until a few moments later that I realized Serena had no problem calling *me* into the fray, and by that time there were more important things to focus on than my hurt feelings.

"Let's get you inside and comfortable, then you can

tell us what happened. It's only a few more steps." I eased her up the porch stairs, unlatched the door with a careless whisper of power, and nudged it fully open with one foot. A low groan issued from Serena's lips and her belly clenched.

"You're in labor." Just stating the obvious.

"Thanks for the clue, I never would have figured that out on my own." Serena panted and nearly broke my fingers when hers convulsed with the pain.

Panicked, I yelled out. "Gran, we have a situation here." Had I just been thinking I could handle things on my own? Silly me.

"What's…Oh." Clara popped around the corner of the fireplace with Aunt Mag close on her heels. "Child, where is your mother?" Calypso Snodgrass might have a reputation for being a cold fish, but none of us could imagine her denying her own daughter the protections and enchantments that can only be passed down through the matriarchal line. There were rituals and rites to make the birthing easier, and given the circumstances, Serena would need all the help she could get.

"Still in the Andes. Coven business," Serena panted. "We had plenty of time when she left."

"I'll get her." Aunt Mag winked out, but as she did, I could see worry etching a few of her wrinkles deeper.

Gently, and with great compassion, Gran brushed Serena's hair back from eyes glazed with terror. "It's going to be okay, Serena. You trust me, right? I know you're scared and tired, but I'm here, and I'll take care of you." Laying both hands on Serena's bulging tummy, Clara concentrated and assessed.

"Is the baby okay? Jett did this to us with some kind of spell. If he hurt my baby, I'll kill him. I don't care what happens to me. He's dead." The mother bear instinct to protect her young loaned Serena the inner strength she would need throughout the coming ordeal.

Patting Serena's arm, Gran assured her, "The baby is fine, just ready to meet mom a little earlier than expected, but there's time yet. Do you understand? All the rituals, all the protections—we have time to put them all in place, so you just hang on, honey. Okay? You'll be cuddling your child soon, concentrate on that joy, and all will be well."

Still, her face could have been carved from granite when she transferred the bulk of Serena's support to her and ordered me to go and tell Terra it was time. I had no idea what rituals and protections Gran was talking about, but Serena seemed comforted, and that was enough for me.

"When this is done, you're going to help me send that jackass somewhere where he can rot for the next century." Flix squirmed under the heat of Serena's glare as Gran helped her into the sanctum where we all waited. "He thought he could mess with my baby, then lock me in my own house. Who does that?"

"How did you get out?"

"Blasted a hole in my bedroom wall. I didn't know I had that much magic in me, to tell the truth. He enchanted all the doors for my protection," her mocking tone put emphasis on the word protection. "I found a book about magical birthing rites hidden under my mattress." Serena's voice rose to the highest pitch I'd ever heard.

"Hush, child. You're safe now." I hoped my grandmother was as sure of that as she seemed. "Terra, you've been through this before, you can handle gathering up what is needed."

A look passed between Gran and Terra that seemed to hold an entire conversation. Terra nodded and took Flix aside. After a short, but animated conversation, he caught my eye, gave me the thumbs up and flickered out to run whatever errand Terra deemed necessary.

Had my birth been such a big deal?

Not wanting to pester Gran with questions at such a delicate time, I turned to ask Salem what he knew and saw his tail disappearing up the stairs toward my room. Before I could follow him, a chiming noise gonged through the house so loud the wave of sound made my teeth clack together, and my chest vibrate. What now?

"Oh!" Evian's exclamation drew my attention to her shocked face. The whole house shook as she rose toward the ceiling and a ball of lightning encased her in a dazzling flash of brilliant white.

What kind of attack puts that look on a faerie's

face? Dazed happiness is the closest I can come to describing it.

"What just happened?" When the light show died down, and Evian returned to the ground, my voice sounded loud in the sudden silence.

"Evian was chosen." Clara clapped her hands in front of her chest and beamed at the happy faerie. In fact, everyone in the room except me was grinning like madwomen while not telling me anything useful.

Times like these, the gaps in my knowledge make me wish I'd listened to Salem and read all the books. "Chosen for what? I don't understand."

"You really are dumb sometimes, Lexi Balefire." Serena could be in labor and still have a sharp tongue. "She's been chosen to serve as faerie godmother to my child." Was that a tear in her eye?

"I'm a true faerie godmother." Joy turned Evian more beautiful than she already was, a feat I never thought possible, and she executed a few graceful dance steps. Then, kneeling before Serena, pledged herself to the baby. A glow erupted around the pair, transmitted something of their emotion to the rest of us. Soleil sobbed with happiness for her sister, and maybe a little jealousy crept into the mix, too.

Before the lovefest got out of hand, Serena galvanized everyone into action with another moan of pain. I felt like a third thumb during the flurry of activity that followed. It seemed everyone except me knew what to do to prepare for the birth, so my assignment was to help Serena walk around until she felt she could no longer stand.

The pacing went on for at least half an hour while the others prepared the sanctuary. No one boiled water. I felt kind of let down that TV and movies had led me wrong on that one.

Compliments of Terra, fresh bedding piled itself into a comfortable pallet over the center of the summoning circle which Gran blessed with a long invocation in the old language. I caught a word or two here and there, but the rest was gibberish to my ears.

No less than four cauldrons bubbled with various brews waiting to be made into potions for healing, health, and protection. Lacking a couple ingredients, Gran prevailed upon the Fae to do their thing. Pots magically filled with dark, rich soil, into which Evian poured a spout of enchanted water that sparkled with rainbow colors. Soleil set miniature suns above each pot and stepped back to let Terra bring forth life.

Seeds shot out the tips of her fingers, arrowed into the pots, and then, like an orchestra conductor, she stood before the row, lifted her hands and funneled earth magic. The germ of life inside each seed responded to her call, to the affirming properties of Fae magic, uncurled, stretched, and burst thin shells to put down roots.

The bow played along with Terra's movements, a

properly enchanting tune that made me grin from ear to ear as the first shoots tested the air above the soil. Tendrils danced up like snakes rearing their heads until, with a final flourish, Terra brought them to full bloom. Leaves sprouted like fireworks. I tell you, watching a master make magic never gets old.

Conversation flowed around me while I turned my focus back to Serena and concentrated on keeping her moving for as long as she could, pausing while the pains rippled through her. The hand that grasped mine seemed too thin, but squeezed hard enough it felt like my fingers might snap.

"You're okay. I've got you." I muttered a litany of soothing comments while she panted and gritted her teeth. "I'm here. You're not alone."

"I want my mom," she said.

"Mag's on it. If there's anyone who can get her here in time, it's my aunt. She's like a bulldog when it comes to getting the job done."

We made a few more rounds of the room before Serena stumbled, cried out, and a gush of liquid hit the floor. "My water broke." Before I had time to think what to do next, she reached out to clutch at my other arm, her eyes rolled back in her head, then reoriented on mine. The look in them chilled me to the bone.

"Oh no. Oh, Lexi, we never found the family talisman. What am I going to do? This is the worst thing that could happen. It's all for nothing." The mother-to-be sagged toward the wet floor.

"Um, Gran. We've got a situation here. I could use a little help." Vaeta reacted first, sent a jet of air to hold Serena up, another to dry the birthing fluid from the folds of her skirt and floor.

"She's okay." With extreme gentleness, Gran ran hands over Serena to assess possible injury or distress. "What happened?"

I passed Serena into waiting Fae arms, repeated the warning she'd given, and explained how she'd nearly fainted. "She didn't want to tell you before because there was plenty of time, but she hasn't been able to find the Snodgrass equivalent of the Stone of Blood. I helped her ransack her house the other day, but the thing never turned up. I feel like there's something going on between Serena and Calypso or she would have just asked her mother where to look."

Hands busy with mixing potion ingredients, Clara sniped. "Calypso Snodgrass is so uptight, I bet her farts have to turn sideways to sneak out."

"Gran, that's…" Hilarious was what it was, and probably all too true. "…not very nice."

"It should have been given to Serena when she Awakened. That's tradition. The vessel that holds each family's ancestral blood is different. Ours is an amulet because the Balefire women have an affinity for stone and metalwork. The Blankenship witches have always been potters, so theirs is a teapot."

Well, that explained some things. "A red one shaped like an elephant?"

"How did you know?"

"Um…I'm not sure. I must have overheard someone talking about it." No wonder the ghost of Tansy Blankenship had been hellbent to retrieve that very same teapot from the repository where dangerous magical things are kept. But I wasn't about to tell the story of my Halloween haunting to my grandmother now. There were other, more important things to worry about.

"Is it a witch thing to require the talisman during a birth or a demigod thing? Maybe Serena left out certain bits of information when she talked to her mother about the pregnancy."

"Demigod. Oh, I see what you're getting at, and it makes sense if Serena hid the information given the way Calypso acted when your mother turned up pregnant. Between you and me, she's quite the snob. You're going to have to go over there and fetch it for me, but don't go alone. Is that Fiach still around?"

Wondering why she'd want Delta in on this, I yanked my phone out of my pocket and shot off a text. Yeah, bounty hunter for the gods used modern technology. Shouldn't come as a surprise.

"Good. Take her with you. Salem, too."

Not that I was complaining, but I had to ask. "You're not trying to get rid of us, are you?"

Orange mist belched out of the potion Gran was stirring, and she held up a hand for silence while she stopped and moved the spoon backwards as if undoing the last three turns. Then she said, "Just be careful. And hurry. Nothing is normal about this birth. I need you back here in time."

"I can't promise anything, I have no idea where else to look?"

"Good thing I used to be coven leader, then isn't it?" Leaning close Gran whispered the location in my ear, and a grin split my face.

"Really? Tell me you're serious."

"As a heart attack."

I had to know. "However did you learn that tidbit of information?"

"A story for another time. Take this." She handed me a glass ball filled with swirling mist.

"What is it?" It paid to ask when Gran pulled something out from up her sleeve.

"Bottled wall. Toss it into the hole to secure the house when you leave."

"Serena, do you have your house key? I'm going to go find your talisman."

She raised an eyebrow at me and I like to think the sarcasm distracted her from the pain for a moment. "I think you'll manage to find a way in given there's a huge hole in the side of the house."

"Oh yeah, brain cramp. Just keep your legs crossed

until I get back." My joking tone and willingness to help released a little of the tension from Serena's body, her shoulders settled into a less hunched position, and she let out a small sigh of relief.

Chapter 19

I had just turned toward the fireplace, noticed the door stood open and Salem's human form was framed in the opening when Flix materialized in front of me and I slammed into his chest so hard it knocked Mag's glass ball out of my hand. Lucky for me Vaeta was watching; she snagged it out of thin air with, well, thin air.

"Oof." My teeth clacked together. The man's body was harder than a stone wall. "Dude, there's such a thing as working out too much."

"Never." He brushed me off like I was a little kid who had taken a tumble, and handed a leaf-wrapped parcel to Terra, who waved it around and did the kind of happy dance that on anyone else would look dorky, but on her, looked like it should be happening on a stage in front of adoring fans. Male fans, that is.

Once he'd handed off his burden, Flix grabbed my arm and kept me from ducking through the sanctum door.

"Where are you going?"

"Serena's place. Delta's on her way to pick me up, and I'm in a hurry. It's urgent."

"I'm going with you." He raised his voice and repeated. "I'm going with Lexi unless you need me for protection here."

Gran waved a hand over her shoulder to hurry us along.

"I'm not scared of Jett, but you're welcome to come along if you want to. They'll be fine here. The godmothers have this place warded so tight a mosquito couldn't slip past."

"No, they don't. Serena can't be inside a warded space while she's giving birth. Not to a Fate Weaver baby, anyway." Did everyone know the protocols except me?

"I had no idea."

Salem opened his mouth, no doubt to point out what I already knew, that I was behind on my reading. Still.

"Don't even think about it." I cautioned him. "There's no time for a lecture."

"I wasn't going to lecture you. I just came to say Delta's waiting in the kitchen."

Flix gentled his voice when Serena whistled out a short cry of pain. "She's terrified, Lexi. Let's hurry."

Calypso and Aunt Mag slid into sight just as I

ducked out the fireplace behind Flix with Salem on my heels. Mag caught my eye, noted my dead-set expression and the determined looks of my companions, and held up a finger. I paused long enough for her to reach into her tie-dyed fanny pack—don't get me started on that—and toss me a small disk. At first, I thought she'd thrown me a coin, but a quick glance showed hand-carved runes decorating both sides, and the level of power coming off the thing made my fingers vibrate.

"Protection." She mouthed. I nodded my thanks, pocketed the charm, and hurried to catch up with Flix. I found him deep in discussion with Delta that ended when they saw me come around the corner.

Only a few short blocks, the ride on Delta's bike wasn't long enough to put me in a Zen state. Not with Salem's claws digging into my leg, anyway. Flix popped into place as we pulled up to the curb.

"I'm waiting out here." Salem refused to step one foot in Serena's house. "I'll stay behind and guard the exit." It sounded noble, but I knew it was because her familiar had a thing for him and Morana might be inside.

We ducked through the hole in the wall, and I made my way down the short hall.

The talisman was right where Gran said it would be. A small, hand-bound book with a leather spine and silver clasp. Totally appropriate for the Snodgrass family since they were born bookworms.

Wrapped in four layers of oilcloth, dropped in a

plastic bag, spelled to blend into any background, and submerged in the toilet tank of the downstairs powder room was an odd choice of hiding place, though. Calypso had resorted to severe measures to keep Serena from laying her hands on the family talisman and I wondered why.

"Are you sure that's it?" Delta eyed the palm-sized book suspiciously. It hadn't taken four of us to retrieve the thing, and why everyone had been so keyed up about it was beyond me.

"Fits the description and was hidden in the right place." I slid the book into my pocket. "While we're here, I want to gather up some things for Serena. I think she'd feel better if she had a change of clothes, her own robe, maybe. And I'm betting there are baby clothes around here somewhere even if she wasn't totally prepared."

Working quickly, and with help from Delta, I packed a bag with things that I hoped would make Serena feel more at home.

"Lexi. You'd better get out here." Salem called through the gaping wall.

"I'll go." Flix vanished and returned just as quickly. "Jett's coming. He has Kin."

Jett had Kin. The way Flix said those words turned my insides to ice, and with the chill came a sense of clarity and purpose. Anger is hot and red and pulsing. Fury is cold and hard and just exactly what I needed at that moment.

I loved the man, but he was a magnet for my enemies. If I'd known bringing on my powers would pull every whack job in the universe out of the woodwork and aim them at Kin, I'm not sure I would have gone through with it.

Ice coated everything except the burning desire for justice. Jett might be a demigod, but the only power I'd ever seen him display with any dexterity was his inherent ability to lodge like a splinter in my backside.

What made him think he could take me on and win? He'd tried before and failed. I carried the Bow of Destiny, I was a Balefire witch. I was more than a match for…

Self-righteous ego carried me through Serena's small house, toward the ragged wall, then melted like cotton candy on a child's tongue when I glanced out the floor-to-ceiling bay window in the dining room.

Through the glass, I saw Jett stalking down the sidewalk, maybe a half a block away. Even from this distance, I could tell Kin was hurt. His body hung with the lip grace of someone who'd been knocked out. As the gap closed between us, I spotted a bruise blooming around one eye and a small cut on his forehead.

The man I loved had been attacked even when he didn't love me back. The sound of blood pumping through my veins roared in my ears, my hair lifted to float around my head in the static haze of magic seeping out of my pores.

One keening crystal note sounded in my head, and I couldn't say if it was my magic or the Bow of Destiny that directed pure sound toward the fragile panes and blasted window glass to dust that fell like a curtain.

I stepped through the frame to face the dark side of my family.

"Delta, will that sword of yours do us any good?" I'd take it from her if I needed to. Jett was mine.

"It'll cut." The sword slid out of its scabbard with a ratcheting sound that alone was enough to strike fear into anyone with half a brain. Not that I thought my half-brother fell into that category. "Skin, and certain types of enchantments. If it has to, Fury will kill."

I had to ask. "Fury?"

"Every great sword has a name. Excalibur, Anduril, Sting."

"The Sword of Gryffindor," Salem tacked his favorite on the end of the list and earned himself a poke in the ribs from Flix.

"What? Harry Potter is a modern classic. Just because Lord of the Rings has been around forever…"

"Shut up, Salem. Does this look like the ideal time for literary debate?" I put no heat into the caution—my full attention was focused on Jett—and by the time he sauntered to a stop, just a few feet away, I'd forgotten Salem or Flix or Delta existed. There was only Jett and Kin and me.

Without my thinking about it too hard, witchfire sparked to life and blazed between my palms; tongues of flame eager to taste Jett's strength, to pit itself against his flesh or his magic, whichever burned easiest. The fire cared little for the target, only for carrying out the will of my intention whether for good or ill.

The color of the flame flipped between black and red. Either would do.

I gathered myself for the throw.

"Do it, and I'll break his fingers. He'll never play guitar again." Jett's voice held no malice, the statement took on a neutral tone that seemed mild compared to the snapping sound, like dry twigs, when I didn't immediately douse the flames. Kin writhed, but it was Flix who grunted in pain.

Fury rode me as my fire streaked toward its mark.

Jett must have picked up a few tricks during his time in the Faelands. He lobbed the ball of magic back at me and we indulged what amounted to a game of tennis minus the bounce. As if picking up kinetic energy from its travels through the space between us, snapping tongues of witchborn flame grew with each volley until Delta reached out with her sword and cleaved the ball in two. A sizzling sound and a curl of smoke were all that remained.

"What do you want, Jett?" As if I didn't already know.

"Serena, and the clock is ticking on the deal. Take

me to her before the baby utters its first cry, or this one dies." My heart wanted to lodge in my throat, but giving in to the urge to scream and try to take Kin forcibly away would only result in another endless tussle. I needed to keep my head clear, so I forced the worry and fear into the dark recesses of my mind. Freaking out would have to wait.

No surprises in Jett's demand, but if he was that dead set on gaining access to my little niece or nephew, I needed to know why. A doting father does not speak of his child so clinically. Every ounce of my willpower went into ignoring Kin's tortured form and fixing a sneer on my face.

"You've picked the wrong bait, brother mine. Kin and I are no longer an item. It seems you're out of the loop." A half-truth, one I had to force off my tongue. Anything to pull Jett's focus off Kin long enough to figure out my next move.

"Sorry Lexi, I've got to…" A shrieking wind sucked the rest of Delta's words away and took my breath along for the ride. The scream of our passage tore the sky on our way to wherever she'd taken us. Or not all of us, Flix and Salem remained behind either by accident or design.

A shock traveled through the soles of my feet when they made contact with solid rock. "Where are we?" My voice sounded strangely flat, almost alien.

"Same place, different dimension." Sweat glistened

on Delta's brow and dripped with a syrup-like consistency. "Delaying tactic, only good for a short time, so quit faffing around."

If Delta's purgatory was a place where little artifice survived, it meant she'd brought me here for one reason, to show me some truth about Jett I needed to see. Once I forced myself to focus on him, the flat light revealed Jett's karmic x-ray. Showed the scared, lonely boy huddled inside the man. For a split second, I mourned the relationship we could have had if he'd come to me with anything other than jealousy and hate for that which had never been under my control.

As it was, I had no shred of compassion left to give. Jett had more than earned whatever might happen to him this day.

What did Jett see when he looked at me in the light of this place of truth? A sister, an adversary? Or did he see the witch and the Goddess who shared my skin? His face gave away nothing. Now that I understood what this place could show me, I wished for a mirror but contented myself with a casual glance at Kin.

There was no Kin, only the vision of a card from Diana Diamond's Tarot deck followed me back when Delta let go of her hold on the place between worlds, and we landed in chaos.

Rather, we landed in the middle of a coup staged by Flix and Salem to get Kin to safety. A coup that looked a lot like an offensive trap play.

Flix ran interference while Salem, tossing a potion bottle at Jett's feet, blitzed the field. He bounced off one of the lawn chairs onto the table to gain added height and executed a flying tackle worthy of the ones that came at the end of every episode of Diagnosis Murder. Salem had a thing for Dick Van Dyke, so he never missed the reruns.

Whatever was in the potion bottle created a cloud of noxious purple smoke that put Jett into a fit of coughing just long enough for Salem to make contact with Kin's limp body. Flix made a shoving motion with one hand, and both Salem and Kin winked out of sight.

"Touchdown," Flix shouted and did his end zone dance while the smoke cleared to show a stunned Jett minus his bargaining chip. The smug look fell off his face in slow motion as he pondered his next move, but there was nothing slow about him when he lunged for the Snodgrass family talisman poking out from the top of the bag I'd packed for Serena. Flix moved like lightning, but he was still too late.

When Delta snaked a length of golden rope around Jett's wrists, one of the writhing ends clipped the talisman, wrenching the silver clasp free of the leather binding.

"Nice work, Wonder Woman." The reference passed over her but elicited a chuckle from Flix.

"You can't do this to me. I need to get to Serena and the baby. Lexi, please. You have to let me see them." As if I would fall for his fake nice face after the way he'd already played me once. To think I'd almost forgiven him.

My hard look did all the talking for me, and Jett went from pleading to threatening.

"Don't you know who I am? My father will smite you like a grape." The more furious his struggle, the tighter Jett's bonds became.

"Don't you mean squash?" I asked.

"Why would anyone smite a gourd?" While I tried to follow the fruit and vegetable references, Delta tied the other end of the rope around her own wrist. "That will keep him until it's time to go."

"Go? Where do you think you're taking me? You have no authority over me, I'm a demigod. My father will…"

Delta yanked Jett toward her with a vicious motion of her wrist, then she insulted him even more by flicking him on the end of his nose. The look on his face was snort-worthy.

"You are an arrogant…" Another flick. "Jackass with an inflated ego…" Flick. "Who possesses neither the wit nor the common sense to use what little power he commands for anything useful. Your father would have sent me after you himself were he able to do so." Another flick. "Now shut up, or I will zip your lip for a hundred years."

Time was running out and worry rode me hard, but

I had to know. "What's going to happen to him?"

Delta appraised him with a haughty look. "Oh, I don't know. I thought I'd give him to the furies. They're the best at teaching naughty boys a lesson."

While she explained, I'd been gathering the pieces of broken talisman. "Bring him back with us now, and if this can't be repaired, you can make sure the furies fit the punishment to the crime. If my mythology serves, I believe they're particularly protective of mothers, so I'm betting they'll take a dim view of what he's done to Serena."

"Speaking of..." Flix reached for my hand and for Delta's then whisked us back home with Jett trailing along behind.

Chapter 20

"Did you get it?" Red-faced and sweating, Serena panted at me the second she saw me step out of the fireplace. "Tell me you found it."

"I did." Telling her the talisman was in pieces seemed unusually cruel, so I squeezed her hand, and the second her focus fell off me, caught Aunt Mag's attention. "You're doing great, Serena." I looked to my grandmother for clarification, and she nodded but continued on with the ritual chanting. Her voice sounded hoarse. "I'll be right back, okay. You're doing great." I repeated because Serena seemed to need the reassurance.

When I got Mag away from prying ears, I said, "It was right where Gran said it would be. The last place Serena and I would ever have thought to look. What does that say about Calypso?"

"Shh. Be careful what you say about her, she's right over there. Give it to me?" I showed Aunt Mag what had happened when Delta and Jett came to blows.

She inspected the damage. "Where is that sniveling weenie. I'm going to give him donkey ears and a set of elephant balls for this."

While the mental image was eminently satisfying, we didn't have time for revenge at the moment.

"Can you fix it?"

Shrugging, Aunt Mag yanked the zipper on her fanny pack and rummaged around in there until she found what she wanted: a jeweler's loupe, which she fitted to one eye.

"He really did a number on it, didn't he? I'm adding a set of boobs to the list of stuff I'm going to do to him. Three of them. I think. Maybe another set on his back."

Stifling the snort, I repeated, "Can you fix it?"

"I'll do what I can." A grim promise. "I'll need Calypso, so send her over here, keep Serena calm, and let me work on it. We're running out of time."

Doing as she asked, I returned to the summoning circle and assured a harried-looking Calypso I would take her place. I'd never seen the woman look so vulnerable as she did with mussed hair and eyes burning a hole in her pale face. A little break from watching her daughter in the throes of labor might help regain her composure.

"I've got her. You go see Mag." It was hard work to keep from yelping when Serena's fingers closed over mine like a vice. Minutes or maybe hours passed before Clara announced it was time to start pushing, but the baby's head crowned quickly after that.

A few vague curses issued from the workbench where Mag and Calypso fought to restore the blood receptacle Clara would need in the next few minutes. One by one, the faeries were called over to work their magic on the elements that made up the talisman. I'd have rather been watching that process than this. Birth is said to be a beautiful thing, but if you ask me, the only people who say that are the ones who get to go home with a baby.

"I think you should let the man speak to his woman." I hadn't heard Vaeta step up behind me. Not an unusual occurrence since she practically walked on air. "He has a truth to tell."

"I'm not his woman," Serena hissed. "Not after what he did to me."

"Are you so certain his motives were evil that you won't even hear him out?"

"Why are you defending Jett? After everything he's done to me, to Kin. Kin. Oh, my Goddess. Where is Kin?" I was mortified I'd become so caught up in Serena's drama, I'd forgotten about him and Salem. "Where's Salem?" Handing Serena off to Vaeta, I rose from her side and rushed over to Flix who apparently agreed with me about the beauty that was the birthing process considering he was in the farthest spot from it he could find.

"It's okay, Lexi. I sent them to County General."

"But Terra could have…" Well, of course, Terra couldn't have helped heal Kin right now. Not with Serena about to deliver at any time. "Never mind. You did the right thing."

"Salem will stay with him."

Swallowing around the lump in my throat, I nodded, and Flix gave me a one-armed hug. One crisis at a time. Story of my life lately.

As crises go, this one shaped up to be a list-topper. With Jett straining at his bonds, godmothers and elder witches chanting while Aunt Mag frantically worked to repair the talisman in time, I felt like I should be in four places at once.

"Lexi, I need you." Aunt Mag tossed the command over one shoulder. The Snodgrass talisman appearing good as new should have erased the wrinkles of worry from her forehead. "Look at this. Waste of time and magic."

"It looks perfect to me, what's wrong with it?"

"Lost too much of the family essence and there's no time to recharge it with enough blood to make it reliable. Not even the best skimmer in all of witchdom could get the job done in time."

"Well, Calypso's right here, can't she—I don't know—top it off with her blood?"

"We'd need at least three more blood ties to make it

strong enough. There is another way, but I don't think Serena will be happy about it."

"I'm a little fuzzy on this whole process." Aunt Mag and Salem's you-don't-study-enough faces are remarkably similar. There must be a trick to raising your eyebrow and squinting at the same time. "Yeah, yeah. I know. I should have read up on interspecies births. Is it for binding?"

"I don't have time to be teaching you lessons you should have already learned, young lady," Mag lectured. "That familiar of yours ought to be spending less time chasing tail and more time on your studies." I wanted to snort at the chasing tail reference, but then I realized she meant it in the cat context, not the human one and it made more sense.

"What can I do?"

Aunt Mag's gaze strayed to Jett, who had given up struggling and now stared at the backs of the women clustered around Serena with enough naked longing and misery on his face that I almost felt sorry for him—even after what he'd done to Kin.

"Did I hear Vaeta advocating for Jett earlier?" She asked.

"Why are you changing the subject?" My head spun trying to keep up.

"She's got a soft heart and a willingness to trust that makes her an easy mark." I'll admit I'd taken my opinion from her sisters who all seemed to think Vaeta's air element made her a bit ditsy at times.

"And you're an idiot." Mag shot back.

"Well, thanks for your extra special vote of confidence, and what is the point of this? We should be concentrating on the talisman."

Judging by the way Clara's chanting had increased in speed, it sounded like we were getting close to the birth.

Still poking her point, Mag asked. "Upon what evidence did you base this theory? She was right about Rhys, wasn't she?"

"Um, yeah. I guess she was."

"If she says he," Mag indicated Jett with a nod of her head, "has something of value to say, she's probably dead on."

"Okay, I'll tell Delta to let him talk, but what does that have to do with this?" I waved a hand toward the repaired talisman.

"Strongest Fate Weaver in history and dumber than a box of rocks sometimes." Eyes rolling up to the heavens, Aunt Mag dropped a knowledge bomb on me. "Did you really think it's all about hearts and love? That you're matching people so they can have a magical kiss and live happily ever after and that's all there is to it?"

"No. Okay, maybe I did, but not anymore."

"Idgit. Did it never occur to you that man," she waved toward Jett, "plus woman," then toward Serena, "equals baby?"

"Come on, I'm not that naive. I do know where babies come from."

To my utter shock, she flicked me on the forehead very much like Delta had done with Jett earlier.

"You're mixing blood with blood. Combining this power with that to make what's needed in the world. Humans may not have magic, but if you think they don't have power, you've been lax in studying history. Hitler had parents. So did Mother Theresa. Sure, there's merit in the nature vs. nurture theory, but it starts with the blood. Different parents, different baby."

A lot of things tried to click into place in my head. Things about Diana Diamond and about the match that I'd felt so strongly compelled to make, but I didn't have time for following through with the enormity of what it all meant. Especially not now, not with Serena's breathing whistling through the air and the need to fix the situation we were in right now.

"Okay, I get that I've been missing some of the finer points of Fate Weaving. What do you expect when all I get are riddles and hints about what I'm supposed to do? But I can't see what all that has to do with the problem at hand. The baby is coming, it's a little too late now to be worried about preventing or fostering the right genetics."

"Blood, Lexi. Think about it. The baby carries Jett's blood and Serena's and all that have gone on before." A surprisingly strong hand clutched my arm, given the frailty of my aunt's appearance. I keep forgetting her age was magically enhanced. Her touch triggered one of my visions. Not the kind that plays like a movie in my head, but the symbolic kind.

Lines formed from light appeared above the heads of everyone in the room. They reminded me of the lines connecting boxes on a flow chart. Yellow lines connected the four faeries and Flix. Blue connected Mag and Clara to me. Pink ran from me to Jett and Jett to Serena. Green laced between Serena to her mother. A second strand of pink joined me to the baby via Jett.

"Oh, I see. I'm connected to the baby through Jett, and since Jett's connected to Serena, we could use the Balefire talisman, right? But wouldn't that have consequences?"

"Now she's catching on. Not as a primary focus, but I think it would provide the added strength. Only there's a drawback…"

You don't have to beat me over the head with a point, I'm not a dunce. "The connection between Jett and me will come into play, and you don't think Serena will go for it. Is there another option? What happens if we don't try it and hers doesn't hold?"

"Wild magic."

"Like a Raythe?"

"Worse. So much worse. There will be consequences for the baby, though. Fate Weaver-type consequences. And I think Vaeta was right that Jett has something to say about all this. Something important. We're going to have to let him talk."

As much as I hated to admit it, Aunt Mag had a point. "Go tell Delta to let up on the reins a little. She needs to still keep a leash on him, though. I'll go prepare Serena for what's coming. Tell Jett he needs to talk fast."

Strong magic rode the air, I could feel it gathering and condensing. If I wasn't mistaken, the baby was about to arrive. Mag handed me the talisman and hurried toward Delta and Jett while I turned back to the center of the summoning circle.

Stepping over the outer ring reminded me of the time our school had taken a field trip to a sheep farm, and I'd accidentally brushed up against the electrified fence. Not a pleasant sensation.

Leaning down, I whispered in Vaeta's ear, "I've got it from here. Stay close, though, we're going to let Jett speak."

"Listen to him with an open heart, please? Trust me on this."

"I'll try. He hurt Kin."

"I know. Hear him out, anyway." Like a puff of smoke, Vaeta faded back, leaving me to kneel and stroke Serena's damp brown hair.

"Honey, I know you're tired, but it's almost over. I need you to listen, now." I caught Calypso's eye to include her in the conversation. She couldn't have been comfortable in the position she'd taken behind Serena to lend support, so I called a couple sofa cushions to pile behind her and received a grateful nod. Everyone had been so focused on the baby, no one noticed the strain on Calypso's face or her veritable silence throughout the process. This was her only daughter and not a regular birth.

"There was a little scuffle when I went back to your place for this," I showed her the book with the silver clasp, "and it broke. Aunt Mag fixed it," I reassured when panic set in. "It's just…it's not quite strong enough for what we need it to do. We're going to refresh your blood ties to the talisman, and that will help, but we need more, so it's a good thing Jett is here."

Serena muttered something under her breath that would have been a curse if she'd had any spare power to put behind it.

"I know. I feel the same way about the jerk. There's more. Since Jett and I share blood, we can use the Balefire talisman in tandem with yours. Is that okay? I already love the baby like family, and you, too." I was surprised to find out I felt that strongly.

"Yes, do whatever you need to do." My fingers creaked under the pressure of hers when another birthing pain made her bear down on them. "And Lexi, hurry. You need to hurry."

I motioned for Jett to come closer, and for Terra to make space for him, but I also noticed Mag pulling out her wand. Let Jett try and pull something, Mag was more than his match.

"Thank you. Thank you. I'm sorry, I didn't mean to break the book, and I'm sorry I hurt Kin. I didn't know what else to do because I didn't think you'd let me in, and all I wanted to do was see my baby. Everything changed when I found out I was going to be a father. I want to change, I swear it."

"He's telling the truth," Vaeta assured.

"I don't care." Goddess love her, Serena let go of my hand, reared back, and landed a well-aimed punch. Jett's nose fountained blood, and I heard cheering inside my head. "How could you do this to me? The nursery isn't ready. Now there's a giant hole in the house, and most of all, you lied to me about wanting to be the kind of father you didn't have. I believed you, you jerk, and then you used magic on me to make the baby come before its time."

"Oh, baby. I'm sorry. I had to do it, but I should have trusted you enough to tell you why. From the minute I knew you were pregnant, I've thought of nothing else, but how best to protect you and the baby from…"

Another pain rippled through Serena, this one stronger than any that had come before. Clara glanced up at Mag. "It's time."

"Lexi, the talisman, hand it to me, please."

One hand still clutched by Serena, I handed off the

one and used the other to yank the Stone of Blood amulet from around my neck, but it was the Snodgrass one she wanted.

"Ouch!" The exclamation slipped out when Mag pierced my finger to mingle my blood with Serena's and those who had come before. She did the same with Calypso and Serena. When she approached Jett, he stood impassively and let her dip into the blood pooling on his upper lip.

"Thank you," he mouthed, and Aunt Mag nodded her head slightly in response. I vowed to tear the Sanctum apart to find more information about Fate Weaver births. So much had happened that I didn't understand.

With each addition, the talisman glowed brighter, and when Mag pressed the anointed object into my hand where I still held the Balefire amulet, the pair dazzled my eyes. Raw power poured over and through me, touched the Goddess and redoubled. My head echoed with the feel of it.

On a low scream, Serena announced, "The baby is coming," and Clara started up the chanting again. To my surprise, Jett joined in. Serena might not have forgiven him, and I certainly had no intention of doing so, but for now, he was part of what I hoped would be a miracle and not a nightmare.

There was a rush, a piercing sense of teetering on the brink of a mile-long fall, and then I heard the first lusty cry from the newborn babe. The Goddess guided my hand, still holding the light-filled conduits of blood magic, to the wet brow of my new nephew.

Bow-song swelled, turned the invocation into a song. I think I'm the only one who saw what happened next, and then, only because of my connection to my father. Slack-jawed and wide-eyed, Jett shook like a leaf in the wind as the baby's wild magic blew through him as though testing his potential before turning to Serena and doing the same.

I realized I wasn't the only one in the know when Evian cast a water dome over the group to contain the untamed power and the other three faeries added their own elements. Inside the protected space, magic tickled over my skin, measured me, caressed my cheek fondly, and quested on. The whole thing lasted a couple of seconds at most but was one of the more intense sensations I've ever experienced.

Glittering twinkles rained down over the baby and Serena. It was then that I noticed Jett lying senseless on the floor, but no one seemed inclined to help him as the magic funneled into his child with a sigh. Clara laid the babe in its mother's chest, and Serena began to glow. Not with residual magic, but with the absolute purity of a loving mother.

The dome of elements popped in a shower of rose petal confetti that melted on contact rather than littering the space.

"A walk in the park compared to the last time we did this, eh?" Clara and Terra exchanged the kind of smile that suggested they'd accomplished something great. "It really went very well, all things considered."

What on earth had happened on the day I was born? One of these days I was going to have to pin my grandmother down and get the gory details.

For the first time ever, Serena resembled her name. Calm-faced, and absolutely glowing, she cradled the baby gently, leaned back into her own mother's warm embrace. Looking at them now, I wondered if Calypso's aloofness had more to do with fear for her daughter than anything else. A smile split her face, transformed her eyes from their normal cool tones to a warm twinkle. A doting grandmother in the making.

"Do you mind?" Clara did not try to take the newborn, she merely waved her hands over him, and when she was finished, Serena held a clean baby wrapped in a warm blanket.

"Thank you. For everything." Heartfelt words from

Serena.

"My pleasure. Now, you'll want to hand him to Evian for her special blessing while we take care of the final details."

I didn't get to see that part because Delta collared me to help her with Jett while Serena delivered the afterbirth.

"Wakey, wakey." I envied Delta giving the new father a few not-so-gentle slaps to bring him around. "It's time to go."

"So you're still taking him away?"

"He's committed several crimes against his own. You, the baby. There are crimes against humans he needs to answer for, but I suspect his sentence will not be as harsh as it would have been given the events today. Consider it a rehab period, if you will."

During Delta's explanation, Jett blinked away the fog, and when he saw my hard expression—despite his supposed change of heart, I mustered up very little forgiveness—his face fell.

"You're right to hate me, Lexi. I deserve no pity from you, and I ask none. Just know I'll find a way to make it up to you somehow. And to Kin. I am sorry for what I've done."

"It's the truth." Her element of air must carry all words to Vaeta's ears because she called out from the other side of the room. I'd have to remember that about her in the future. A faerie with super hearing might come in handy. Or annoying, depending on the situation.

Turning to Jett, I addressed him finally, "If Kin suffers any lasting damage from your actions today, I'll…"

"I really am sorry."

"Even so, you're not forgiven yet." To Delta, I said, "Give him a minute with Serena and the baby before you take him off to what I hope is a worthy sentence. He should at least get to kiss his son before he goes."

Jett cradled the baby gently and leaned in, then looked up at Serena, his eyes pleading, "What is his name?"

"Kaine. Kaine Striker." Tears formed in the corners of Jett's eyes as he bestowed a kiss on his son's forehead, his finger trailing over the babe's cheek in a gesture so filled with pure, gentle love that I almost had to look away.

"Thank you, Serena. You have no idea how much this means to me." Jett collected himself and deposited one more kiss on Serena's forehead before resigning himself to his fate. "One more thing. Take this," Jett reached under his shirt, pulled out a small stone affixed to a leather strap and held it out to me.

"What is it?" Excuse me if I still didn't trust the jerk, I had good reasons.

"Honestly, I'm not sure. The Fae I got it from said it would help me find our father, but I couldn't get it to work. Maybe you'll have better luck with it."

"Yeah, okay. Um, thanks, I guess." Don't ask what made me do it, but I pulled Mag's protection charm from my pocket and handed it to him in trade.

Since it seemed my work here was done, it was time to clean up and go check on Kin. I hit the shower, changed clothes, and headed for the hospital where the next wrinkle in my day waited.

If I'm honest, I still had no idea how to break Diana's hold on Kin, but I was riding the high of helping Serena through a fairly seamless demigod birth and felt as though nothing could stop me now. With little time to process what I'd seen in Delta's vision, of one thing I was sure: Diana was, indeed, the Darkest Heart, and even though I loathed the idea of trusting anything that came from my mother's mouth I knew in my Fate Weaver gut she was telling the truth.

The Kin who loved me was inside there, somewhere, and I was running out of time. If I already had what I needed to defeat Diana, dilly-dallying around to figure out a plan could run the timer down to zero. My only option was to wing it and hope my improvisation skills would kick in at the opportune moment.

Diana, if my calculations were correct, carried only a quarter share of Psyche's blood plus whatever extra strength she gained from the Tarot cards. Between them, they might even out the playing field against any other

Fate Weaver—but not me. The time had come to live up to my potential.

There was a vial of invisibility draught safely tucked into the messenger bag I'd grabbed before sneaking out of the house. The potion would provide unimpeded entrance to Kin's hospital room since visiting hours were long over. I couldn't take the chance of skimming in; appearing out of thin air in front of humans is strictly forbidden.

Swallowing the clear liquid in one gulp, I felt a trickle of magic begin to spread from the top of my head all the way to the tips of my toes, my body disappearing inch by inch on its way down. I sidestepped the meager hospital staff tending the night shift, and prepared to search behind the reception counter for Kin's room number when a familiar, frigid chill stole my breath away.

Caution thrown to the wind, I followed the chill and burst through Kin's door to find the essence, but not the body of Diana Diamond standing over Kin, her head bent low, preparing to devour whatever dregs of dark energy her magic had loosed into the world.

"No!" The exclamation lurched and caught in my throat, and I lunged toward her with witchlight shimmering in my palm. Diana burst into ether and reconstituted herself on the other side of the room. I positioned myself between her and Kin, refusing to play a game of cat and mouse I couldn't possibly win in corporeal form.

"It won't change anything, he's still mine. It's too late to break my hold on him," she taunted. I remembered the way Diana had slurped up the darkness she created, and the ick factor made me shudder again. I would not allow her to make a meal out of Kin. "I plan to savor him right down to the last delicious drop."

So there was time, Diana just admitted she wasn't finished with Kin. I thought of the dog-eared card I carried the back pocket of my jeans. Diana seemed fine with gloating, and part of me wanted to let her continue ranting.

"And then what, Diana? You'll finally be allowed entrance to Olympus? I somehow doubt they'll sing your praises for wreaking this much havoc on earth. Do you think you'll be welcomed back with open arms?"

I didn't have a clue in hell what the gods' reaction would be, but I doubted Diana would be considered anything other than a trespassing interloper.

Jackpot I thought, as Diana's eyes narrowed to slits and she pierced me with a hollow, ice cold glare. "Who are you to tell me whether I belong amongst the gods? My mother made the decision to leave Olympus; made it for the both of us before I was old enough to have any say in the matter."

What was it with demigods and parental problems? First Jett, now Diana, and it's no secret my issues with my father could fill a psychology textbook.

"Surely there are other ways to accomplish your goal?" I moved a little closer to Kin while Diana's ghostly form got more and more agitated. "You really feel it necessary to damn all of humanity before you skip town?"

"Humanity. There's a laugh. That true love you believe in so blindly is a lie. You think you're so much better than I am, but for all the store you set by true love's kiss, you should know he was easy to turn to my will, even if his heart is so pure it tastes like poisoned candy to me. Your precious Kin is nothing special, he's just like all the rest of the sniveling horde."

I clamped down on all the hot retorts that wanted to fly out of my mouth. Kin was wonderful and amazing, but I needed a level head if I was going to save the day.

"Wow, that ex of yours really scorned you didn't he?" You know what they say, *hell hath no fury* and all that. I was beginning to wonder if the phrase had been coined for Diana herself.

Diana stopped pacing and stood utterly, disconcertingly still. "How do you know about that? You've been snooping around in my business. What have you Seen?"

"Enough to know you've been working toward your goal for quite some time, and you're about this close," I held up my thumb and forefinger for emphasis, "To getting what you want. But you didn't count on Lexi Balefire causing so many problems."

Fury rose in Diana's cheeks, and I knew I'd hit on a sore spot.

"You won't stop me. Do you hear me, you egotistical bitch? I have few cards left to play, and then you'll pay. You'll all pay." Could she be any more of a cliché?

The room darkened suddenly, and I felt my inner goddess flare to life and settle into my skin like a coat of armor.

There's something about tapping into the deepest part of your inner power that lends a clarity of vision you might only ever experience once in a lifetime. For me, that timeless moment carried a vast feeling of interconnectedness that I never expected. Every atom of me felt tuned into the universe.

Goddess Lexi picked up the bow, and it became a harp. I both saw and became her as she plucked at the strings and played a tune so sweetly perfect that every note held the sum of all experience. For the first time, I had a glimmer of what it might be to fully embrace my inner Fate Weaver. If this was what it felt like to be a god, I could understand why Diana was so tightly focused on ascending to Olympus. No superlative existed in any known language that could come close to describing the delicious power vibrating through me.

I blinked.

The world went all colors and shapes as if I could see the sounds the harp was playing instead of only hearing them. Diana was there, too. A growing stain against the shifting light of perfect being. An abomination. A thing that had been born of light, but chosen the dark and by so doing, had forced away her own soul.

I felt sorry for her. Not much, but enough to turn me into the form of a lesson. A mirror. A literal mirror for her soul.

When she saw herself reflected from my presence, Diana blanched. Her sneer turned into a silent scream, her body to a bird-like thing with greasy wings that tore at the sky, and then she was gone.

Kin's breathing hadn't quickened during the entire confrontation with Diana Diamond, thanks, I assumed, to the steady drip of pain medication flowing from a suspended bag into his good arm.

I placed one of his limp hands in my own, and concentrated on the feel of his guitar string-calloused fingers, remembering how it felt when they tangled in my hair or stroked a tear from my cheek.

The Tarot card Diana had used to curse Kin began to hum with power as I pulled it free of my back pocket, and I knew almost no time remained before its magic would seal our fate.

Bow-song echoed the lingering essence of whatever it was the harp had bestowed upon me, and suddenly an inkling of an idea began to take form. Like the pieces of a puzzle falling into place, snippets of information flooded my memory.

Eris and Aneris were divested of this very same deck of cards when their intentions for the game had been duplicated in the human realm, forcing war and shuttling humanity between order and chaos. And, after all, hadn't the importance of intention been one of Salem's and then Gran's favorite lecture topics?

Your intention guides the spell, Lexi.

Craft your intentions carefully, Lexi or the spell may backfire.

Intentions. Intentions. Intentions.

It was time to put the Queen into checkmate, and I'd already proved myself a worthy opponent. Mona's proclamation that love was always enough echoed through my consciousness, along with Salem's advice about releasing my pain rather than letting it pull me down into its undertow.

The sound of a thousand violins wept in my head while Balefire heat rose up in my belly to fill the hole that threatened to eat me alive. My heart felt like a wild thing in my chest, fluttering against my ribcage, trying to break free.

What wanted to come was a primal scream. One that would burst from my throat, rip and tear it's way free. But this was a hospital and no place for reckless behavior. What came instead were tears.

Tears of sorrow, joy, hope, regret, and most of all love for Kin streamed down my face, dripped onto the

Tarot card in sizzles of white light until the surface glowed and shifted from the Lovers Tarot card to a regular queen of diamonds.

Magic whipped into a frenzy around Kin's body, lifting it off the bed and, filling him with its glow until I had to shield my eyes from the brightness. The inky black of the last of Diana's magic flowed out of him as the light grew dim, and when it disappeared in a shimmer of sparkling dust Kin let out a sigh, "Lexi."

I ripped the card to shreds, tore the shreds to tinier pieces still, and burned the scraps to ash with witchfire, then blew on them to disperse the motes and let the air carry them away.

A streak of soot clung to Kin's forehead when I laid a kiss there and let him sleep.

Chapter 21

I stepped into the kitchen with no idea we had company or I wouldn't have come down in my pajamas and a pair of unicorn slippers.

"That's it, just one more signature and it's yours." The stately woman who Gran introduced as Ellen Blackthorn brandished a ballpoint pen while casting an envious eye at the curvaceous figures of the faeries' human glamours which, even toned down would still put a supermodel to shame. If only she could see the real thing.

Gran scrawled her name with a flourish, then handed the pen to Mag so she could do the same. A cold breeze blew in through the cracked kitchen window and rustled the papers, then settled with an air of finality. The room felt quieter afterward, and a tinge of sadness colored the air.

Ellen passed Gran a set of keys, reminded us gently

that she appreciated referrals, and bustled out the front door.

Upon her exit Salem, Pye, and Jinx blinked back into their human forms, having spent the last hour circling the poor real-estate agent who had tried to politely avoid leaving with her linen slacks covered in cat hair. Her reluctance to pet any of them made the game all that much more fun because many cats just love to approach anyone who shows disinterest and vehemently prefer to avoid those who would love nothing more than a kitty cuddle. Sadists, cats, each and every one of them.

I'd thought all the drama was over when I walked back into the house the night before, but the morning had brought another surprise. One which explained all the secrecy between Gran and Aunt Mag this past couple of weeks.

"Lexi, are you sure you're all right with this?" Gran placed a hand on my shoulder and brushed a stray lock of hair behind my ear with a gentle smile. "We wanted to tell you the minute we decided, but things have been a little hectic around here."

"Does it matter?" I responded, tears threatening to spill over at any second. *I will not cry. I will not cry.*

"It does matter, dear. But I think you know deep down this is what's best. You don't really need us here every day. You have your own life. Your godmothers have their own lives. It's time your Aunt Mag and I had our own lives too.”

“It’s just under an hour away by car, but now that you’ve learned how to skim, you can drop by anytime. It will be like we never left. And you are all welcome to visit anytime you’d like.” Mag nodded to the faeries who so far had maintained as much distance as they were capable, all lined up against the kitchen island.

Terra, always the spokeswoman for the group, stepped forward, “We hope you don’t feel as though we’ve driven you out of your own house. We could find another place ourselves, if you’d rather.”

Aunt Mag laughed out loud, and Gran grinned from ear to ear, “Now that we’ve had time to get used to the idea, we’re quite excited for this new chapter in our lives to begin. I’ve always wanted to own a shop.”

“Explain to me again why it’s necessary that you move to some podunk town in the middle of nowhere?”

“Harmony is not a podunk town. It’s a quaint little place with a thriving tourist trade. We’ve been called in because the local high priestess has descended rather gracelessly into old age. There have been one or two incidents recently,” Mag and Gran exchanged a glance that made me wish they would elaborate. I sensed a funny story there. “And there are concerns about Hagatha stirring up more trouble. They need someone with a firm hand to run the coven, and with a great deal of diplomacy to keep Hagatha from figuring out she’s no longer in charge.” Gran explained for about the tenth time.

"I don't see why this is any of your concern. Why don't they just name a new high priestess?"

Mag, patient for the first time ever, patted me on my arm, "It doesn't work like that dear, and even if it did, Hagatha would never allow herself to be dethroned. Wouldn't be pretty, and we're not in the habit of throwing the baby out with the bath water. Despite her current state, the woman deserves our respect. Besides, Clara and I finally have had a chance to reconnect as sisters. She knows this city life has never been my bag. Too many people. We'll be happier in the country. Now, speaking of being a skim away," she grabbed my wrist in one hand, and Gran's in her other, and with a whoosh, we were no longer standing in the Balefire house kitchen.

When I opened my eyes—because squeezing them shut seemed the rational response to being dragged unexpectedly through space—the sun shone brightly against a sky at least three shades bluer than it ever looked in Port Harbor.

A pair of willow trees, spidery-looking in their current state of nakedness, flanked a crooked brick path leading from a quaint village sidewalk to the front door of the historic two-story building Gran and Mag would now call home. The trees, combined with the yard's gentle downward slope, and an ivy-bedecked wrought iron fence lent an air of privacy to the property, even though it sat smack in the middle of what qualified as the commercial district.

I could make out the words "Odd's Ends" scrawled across a faded, rust-covered sign hanging crookedly above the door, and was morbidly curious what sorts of things had once been sold behind the paper-covered windows. I was also dying to follow the footpath around the back of the house to catch a view of the river that butted up against the edge of the property.

"We'll tidy up the grounds, of course, and it's going to take the lot of us to hoe out the mess that was left behind." Gran wrung her hands and watched my stony face with bated breath.

I sighed, waited a few seconds longer than necessary just for effect, and finally let a wide smile cross my face, "It's lovely. Or, at least, I can see that it will be once you've made it your own. Show me the rest."

Chapter 22

I finally learned that the ease of skimming is directly proportionate to the level of emotion I'm feeling when I try. In other words, it's gut magic. As much as I'd loved watching Gran and Mag explore every nook and cranny of their new property, I couldn't bring myself to say goodbye and just vanished. It was silly; they were literally a wink away, and I wouldn't be surprised to find them in the kitchen every midnight with all the rest of the snack brigade.

Even though they'd only been here a short time, having Gran and Mag around had made me feel closer to my witchy roots than ever before. They were nosy, and they made snide comments about nearly every outfit I put on, but the lack of boundaries made it feel like family. Our connection was innate, and that was something I'd longed to experience my entire life. I would miss them terribly.

What's the best way to put something unpleasant out of your mind? Focus on the positive, and for me, that meant fixing my pathetic love life.

Nervous butterflies danced in my stomach as I made my way up the curved concrete stairway of Port Harbor Community Hospital. Given I'd dosed him with Jett's healing potion, Kin should be getting released anytime, and I'd put on his favorite outfit in preparation for our first post-Diana Diamond encounter.

A denim skirt clung to my hips and skimmed the tops of a pair of knee-high lace-up boots that made my calves look amazing. Fuzzy chenille hugged my arms to the elbows, and the sweater was cut low enough to show off enough but not too much.

I flicked a stray ringlet back over my shoulder as I pushed a pair of tortoiseshell sunglasses on top of my head.

"I'm here to see Mackintosh Clark."

The elderly door attendant trailed an arthritic finger down the list and I shifted my weight from one foot to the other for the approximate ten years it took her to find Kin's name. "Room 212, go ahead down, dear."

Apparently, security wasn't an issue at PHCH after all because nobody cast me a second glance as I turned the corner with bated breath.

"Knock, knock," I said as I rapped my knuckles on the heavy oak door. Why do people do that anyway? You wouldn't punch someone in the face and say "punch, punch" while you did it.

"Come in." The butterflies turned to birds and threatened to fly up my throat and out of my mouth. I swallowed them back down and prepared myself for seeing my beloved soul mate sporting the damage he had undergone during this go-round with my magical karma.

I breathed a sigh of relief when I finally laid eyes on Kin and saw his color was better today. The only indication he'd required hospitalization was a two-inch bandage in the center of his forehead, a splint on one hand, and an IV line hanging running from the crook of his elbow to a rack of fluids at the head of the bed.

I rushed to his side and reached for his hand, stopping short when I realized Kin was staring at me with a confused expression. "Can I help you?"

"Um, excuse me?"

"Are you looking for the guy next door? He's been taken down for more x-rays, but he should be back any minute. What's your name, I'll let him know you stopped by."

"You don't know who I am?" I squeaked.

"Should I?" Kin quipped, the trademark grin lighting his face like a stab in my heart.

Answers whirled in my head, the first of which being a more profane version of "yes," while the pieces of the puzzle clicked together. Flix had said that my Kin was in there somewhere and that I only had a limited time to release him from Diana Diamond's hold before I lost him forever.

I don't know what I thought that meant, but I certainly hadn't thought Kin forgetting about me entirely was a possibility.

"Sorry, I…I'm sorry." Stunned, I stumbled out the door.

It was over. After everything I'd gone through to save him—us—I was too late.

Chapter 23

Curls of dark hair pooled around my feet, and nothing had ever sounded as good as the snick-snick of the scissors while I honed my outer image to match the inner. No more soft and cute and weak. I needed hard edges, straight lines.

Sure, I could have used glamour to style the new do, but it wouldn't have been nearly as visceral or satisfying as the touch of metal creating an angled cut that hit just below my chin. Happy with the length, I shook my head from side to side, sent magic down each strand until the curling mass tamed itself in a shock-white, bone-straight curtain tipped with two inches of hot pink.

A wave of one hand over my face altered the sweet and wholesome makeup to something smoky and dramatic—slashing color sharpened my cheekbones, and the eyes looking back at me from the mirror sizzled.

Anything in my closet that was not black got pushed toward the back. Now that I was in charge of the body, there would be no more cutesy outfits, no more pastels.

Lexi Balefire? I shoved her deep down where the puling and crying over her failed love life would be less of a distraction.

My name is Alexis. A name that means protector. A name fit for a Goddess.

-The End-